JESSICA BECK

THE DONUT MYSTERIES, BOOK 32

BOSTON CREAM BRIBERY

The First Time Ever Published!

The 32nd Donut Mystery.

Jessica Beck is the *New York Times* Bestselling Author of the Donut Mysteries, the Classic Diner Mysteries, the Ghost Cat Cozy Mysteries, and the Cast Iron Cooking Mysteries.

For the two people closest to me on earth,
P and E, now and forever!

When head town councilman Van Rayburn is attacked at his home and left for dead, Suzanne and Jake struggle to prove that their friend, Mayor George Morris, is innocent of committing the assault. The only problem is that there is evidence left at the scene that implicates the mayor, and Van can't seem to remember the attack at all!

CHAPTER 1

THE CHARITY AUCTION WAS SUPPOSED to be for a good cause, but all of our noble intentions didn't matter in the end.

Bidding during the event turned out to be intense, but I had no idea just how dangerous the whole thing would get before it was all over.

"Your donut-making lessons are already going for over a hundred dollars," Momma said as she joined Jake and me at our table in the town hall. We were raising money for the soup kitchen, a cause near and dear to my heart. Momma was in charge of the event, and she'd had the brilliant idea of holding a silent auction where folks from town bid on learning new skills and having unique experiences with local experts. We were currently dining on spaghetti and meatballs, all provided for a modest fee that went directly to the charity as well. Momma didn't miss a beat, and I was surprised she hadn't set up a liquor station as well.

"You're kidding," my husband said before he realized how that must have sounded. "I mean, congratulations."

"How's Jake's storytelling session doing?" I asked. My husband, a former investigator for the state police, was auctioning off a lunch at which he would regale the buyer with tales of his time on the force. I was tempted to bid on it myself, since Jake was usually reticent about sharing information about his time as a police inspector, even with me.

"It's just below seventy dollars," she said as she patted her son-in-law's hand. "Don't worry, Jake. I'm sure someone will step up."

"Hey, seventy bucks just to hear me talk sounds like pure profit to me," my husband said magnanimously.

"You still have to provide the lunch too, you know," I reminded him.

"I've already worked that out," he said smugly. "I managed to procure a donation."

"You didn't talk Trish into feeding you for free, did you?" I asked. Trish Granger, the owner of the Boxcar Grill, was a good friend of mine. She was offering a lesson working the grill with Hilda as her contribution.

"I did one better than that. Barton Gleason agreed to cater it for me last night," he said smugly.

Momma frowned. "Jake, why am I just hearing about this now?"

"I didn't think it mattered," my husband said.

"You're kidding, right? Barton is already catering one meal, and it's up to two hundred dollars so far. Your lunch just got quite a bit more valuable." Momma jumped up from the table and went directly to the microphone. "Folks, I've just learned that the lunch and story time with Jake Bishop will be catered by Barton Gleason."

There were quite a few murmurs from the crowd, and I saw a mad dash for Jake's auction sheet. Barton was dating my assistant, Emma Blake, and he worked at the hospital cafeteria, creating unbelievably great cuisine.

"I'm not thrilled she called it story time," Jake muttered beside me.

"It's getting results. That's what counts," I said. "It's all for a good cause, remember?"

"Sure," Jake said a little sullenly, and then he brightened considerably. "Well, at least it's a race now between us."

"I give up," I said as I waved my white paper napkin in the air. "My donuts are good, but the combination of your tales and Barton's cooking is going to be impossible to beat."

Grace joined us, holding a plate and cup. "Is there room for one more?"

"You bet," I said, scrunching over to make space for her. "How's your makeover doing?" Grace worked for a large cosmetics company, so it was only natural that she was contributing some of her own wares.

"Gabby Williams keeps outbidding everyone else," Grace said with a groan. Grace and Gabby weren't what I'd call close by any definition.

"Seriously? Is there a new man in her life?" I asked.

"Well, I doubt she's doing it for us," Grace said. "Your donut lessons seem to be going strong."

"Who's leading now?" I asked. I wasn't sure why anyone would want to work with Emma and me at Donut Hearts. It would take a real fan to be willing to come in at three a.m. just to learn how to make donuts with us.

"Van Rayburn and George Morris are in a bidding war," Grace said. "They keep trying to one-up each other. It's hilarious."

"I'm not sure it's all that funny," I said. Van and George were natural-born enemies, and I hated that they were using my donuts to go after each other. George was our mayor, while Van was the most vocal town councilman who seemed to oppose him at every turn.

"It's all for a good cause, remember?" Jake reminded me.

"Okay. You're right." I took a bite of spaghetti. "This isn't bad, is it?"

"If you don't mind getting your sauce from a huge can and your pasta being overcooked, it's absolutely delightful," Grace said with a grin. She took a bite from her fork, smiled, and then said, "But hey, it's all for a good cause, right?"

We joined her in her toast, clinking our plastic cups together. "For a good cause," we echoed, and then the three of us started laughing. It earned us a few odd looks from the folks sitting at our table, but I didn't care. I loved being with Grace and Jake and, what was more, being a part of our entire community. It was one of the things I loved best about small-town living.

Momma took the stage and tapped on the microphone a few times. It was enough to get everyone's attention, though I would have had to light the banner on fire to achieve the same result. There was something commanding about my mother that I'd never been able to put my finger on. I certainly hadn't inherited the gene from her.

"Folks, we're down to our two-minute warning, so if there's something you've got your eye on, it's time to make your move."

It was amazing how the activity around the tables holding the auction sheets suddenly erupted with people vying for victories.

"Is there anything you want to bid on?" Jake asked me.

"You won't let me do your lunch. Besides, it's probably out of my league by now. How about you?"

"I've got my eye on something," he said as he stood. "Ladies, if you'll excuse me," he said.

"What's he going to bid on?" Grace asked as Jake left us.

"I have no idea," I admitted. "This is nice, isn't it?"

Grace looked around and nodded in agreement. "I know I joke a lot about it, but I love April Springs. Events like this bring out the best in us."

"And the worst, too," I said as I saw Cynthia Trent and Gabby Williams fighting over an auction sheet, no doubt Grace's offering. "Looks like you're very popular," I said.

"Not as much as Jake is," she said, pointing at another crowd.

I glanced over at my sheet and saw George hovering over

it. It would be fun having him in my shop, and I was glad Van Rayburn had evidently given up.

As Momma started her countdown, Rayburn strolled up to the mayor and laughed. I didn't know what he said to George, but the mayor looked upset as Momma called out, "Time!"

As she started to collect the sheets, I heard George and Rayburn arguing. Shoot, everyone in Town Hall heard them.

"That's cheating," George said loudly.

"I spilled something on the sheet, so I was cleaning it," Rayburn countered, trying—and failing miserably—to sound innocent.

"Why did you have a dummy list here, then?" George asked.

"I didn't do that," Rayburn replied, though it was clear that he'd done exactly that.

"Dot, this isn't right," George protested.

Momma spoke softly to both men, who appeared to nod their heads in agreement, however reluctantly. To my surprise, the three of them then headed straight to my table.

I stood as they approached. "What's going on?"

"Suzanne, would you be willing to teach both of these gentlemen how to make donuts tomorrow morning?" Momma asked.

There was barely going to be enough room for one of them in my kitchen with Emma and me, but I knew better than to cross my mother when she was that determined. "It would be my pleasure," I said, though it was going to be anything but that, especially if the two men bickered as much as I suspected they would.

"Excellent! Problem solved," Momma said, and then she moved back to continue to collect auction sheets before they could say anything else.

"What time do I need to be at the shop tomorrow?" George asked, pointedly ignoring his rival.

"Yes, when should *we* arrive?" Rayburn asked sweetly.

"I start my workday at three a.m.," I said. "I'll see you both then."

"Very well," Van said, though it was clear he wasn't exactly thrilled about my working hours. That was just too bad. I wasn't about to change them just for him.

"Sorry about that, George," I said after the town councilman was gone.

"No worries," the mayor and my friend said. "I doubt the old windbag will even bother showing up."

Given what I'd just seen, I doubted it, but there was no reason to say anything to George. "I'll see you in the morning."

"If you can call six hours from now morning," George said with a grumble.

"Hey, I used to come in at one a.m. once upon a time," I reminded him. "Be thankful for small favors."

"I am," he said, and then he was called away by one of his constituents.

As Momma read off the list of winners and the amounts they'd donated, I watched as Grace cringed when Gabby's name was announced as the winner of her makeover.

"Wonderful," she said acerbically.

"Sorry," I said. Jake rejoined us while Momma was still calling out winners. "How did you do?"

"I got outbid at the last second," he said with a shrug.

"Just out of curiosity, what were you bidding on?" I asked him.

"I wanted to drive one of the town's snowplows," he said glumly.

"In July?" I asked.

"You don't think they'd let me do it in December, do you?" he asked with a grin.

"No, probably not," I answered. After Momma finished reading off the winners, we all cheered and gave ourselves a round of applause before pitching in and cleaning up. After we were finished, I kissed Jake's cheek and said, "By the way, who won your lunch?"

"A local business owner," Jake said. "Well, have a good night." He was being evasive, which was something unusual for my husband.

"Which local business owner?" I asked, standing firm in my spot.

"Ellie Nolan," he admitted.

Ellie was young, attractive, and not afraid to go after married men. She'd taken the gym over when its previous owner, Candy Murphy, had committed murder. Candy had hired Ellie originally to be her second-in-command at the gym, so I wasn't quite sure why it surprised me that the two women were so similar, and in all the wrong ways. "Seriously?"

"She told me she loved Barton's food," Jake replied lamely.

"Let's make sure that's *all* she samples during your lunch," I said.

"Come on. Let's go home," he said as he kissed my cheek.

"No, you stay and have fun," I said. "I can make it back home on my own."

"Honestly, I didn't put her up to it or anything," Jake explained.

"I know that," I said. "No worries. I just don't want you to miss out on the fun."

"The only thing I'll miss is you when you're gone," he said.

Grace laughed beside him. "Wow, that was really smooth, Jake."

He just shrugged as he took my hand. "Let's go home, Suzanne."

"Sounds good to me," I said, pleased that my husband was going with me, not because of Ellie but because I loved his company.

As we made our way home in the warm July night, I watched

as lightning bugs danced all around us. The park was full of them, and they were a delight to walk among.

By the time we made it back to the cottage we shared, I'd almost forgotten about Ellie.

Almost, anyway.

I was not at all surprised to find George waiting for me outside Donut Hearts the next morning, as early as it was. As I fumbled for my keys, I asked, "Any sign of Van yet?"

"I told you he wouldn't show up. He's probably sleeping in," George said with a grin. "It looks like you're stuck with just me."

"I'd never call that being stuck," I said as I found the right key and opened the front door. After a moment, something just didn't feel right about it, though. "You know what we need to do, don't you?" I asked George as I flipped on the coffeemaker.

"Get busy making donuts?" he asked as he rubbed his hands together.

"Not just yet. We need to go get Van first."

George's grimace was all the answer I really needed. "Suzanne, he didn't pay for a wake-up call, too. After all, *I* made it in without help."

"True, but if the roles were reversed, I would have insisted that Van go with me to wake you."

"That's the difference between us," the mayor said. "I wouldn't have needed it."

It was clear that the mayor wasn't all that happy about the prospect of waking up his competition, but I wasn't about to budge. "If you don't want to go with me, suit yourself. You can make yourself at home here. I should only be fifteen minutes, and we'll get started on the first round of cake donuts as soon as I get back."

George's expression clouded up. "Are you really going to go fetch him?"

"I am," I said. "Like I said, you're free to join me, but one way or the other, I'm going. He just lives a few blocks away. We can go on foot, if you'd rather."

"I'll go, but only if you take your new Jeep. I've been waiting for a chance to take a ride in that thing."

"It's a deal," I said, happy that George had folded. I hadn't been looking forward to waking Van without him. As for the new Jeep, I hadn't wanted to part with the old one, but an intentional accident had ruined it, and I'd been forced to buy a new one, much to my chagrin. It wasn't that the new Jeep wasn't nice. It just wasn't my old one, if that made any sense. Jake thought I was crazy, but I'd become attached to the one I'd had all those years, and the new one and I hadn't had any adventures together yet, though I was pretty sure that was going to eventually change. "Hey, think how much fun it will be rousing him from a deep sleep. That's almost like winning another prize at the silent auction."

George laughed. "I never thought of it that way. Do you have an old pan and a wooden spoon I can borrow?" The mayor's expression had gotten suddenly devious.

"Are you really willing to risk irking some of your other constituents by making that kind of racket?" I asked, guessing what he had in mind.

"You bet I am," he said with a wicked little laugh. "If anyone complains, I can blame it all on Van. So, do you have anything I can use?"

I tried not to laugh as I grabbed an old, worn-out pot that I'd been meaning to donate to the soup kitchen, and then I found a wooden spoon that we never used. "How does this setup look?"

"Perfect," he said as he took the newly purposed noisemakers from me and gave them a trial bang. The sound was deafening inside my small donut shop. "Let's go."

We went out to the Jeep, but not before I carefully double-checked to make sure that I'd locked up. On our way out, I'd grabbed a sign for the front door just in case Van showed up while we were gone, so I hung it in place as we left. It simply said, "Back in fifteen," and I'd used it on more than one occasion in the past.

As George and I drove down Springs Drive together in the dark, I said, "I can't believe you're going to disrupt this sleepy little town just to have a little fun."

"Then you must not know me as well as you think you do," George said. I wasn't about to encourage him, but it was nice to see the little kid in him again. Since taking over the mayoral duties for our little town, George's demeanor, never really all that playful to begin with, had definitely taken on a more sedate tone.

"I don't know about that," I said as I parked in front of Van's neat little cottage just past the bank and on the way to the hospital. There was a cluster of other small places near him, all of them quaint. "Are you sure about your noisemaker idea?"

"Just watch me," George said. He popped out of the Jeep, and before I could say another word, he started banging on the bottom of the pot with the wooden spoon. "Wake up, you old coot. It's time to get cracking."

I grabbed the heavy-duty flashlight from my Jeep and pointed it toward the cottage. A few lights flicked on around Van's place, but the cottage itself was still dark.

"The man must sleep like the dead," George said as we approached the front door.

"Or he's already at the donut shop waiting for us," I offered.

"No way. We'd have seen him on our drive over." George

stopped walking and talking kind of abruptly and put out an arm to stop me.

"What's going on?" I asked him, curious about our sudden stop.

"That," George said as he pointed in the direction of the narrow porch. "Shine your light over there, Suzanne."

I did as I was told, and I saw something that looked like spilled chocolate syrup spread out on the concrete. "What is that?" I asked.

"Blood," George said. "I've seen it enough to know it on sight, even in this bad light; there's no mistaking it." He handed me the pot and spoon and said, "Let me see that torch of yours."

I didn't quite just hand it over. "George, I know you used to be a cop, but shouldn't we call the current police chief? Chief Grant is going to want to handle this himself."

"We'll call him as soon as we know what's going on," George insisted. "I still need that flashlight, though."

I wasn't about to deny him, no matter how crazy it felt to be exploring an obvious crime scene without at least having some kind of weapon between the two of us. That wasn't strictly true, I realized as I handed George the heavy flashlight. He had that, while I took over the pot and the spoon. They weren't the worst weapons I'd ever tried to use against a bad guy, but they were certainly in the running.

"Stay out here," George ordered me.

It was a directive I had no trouble ignoring.

When he realized that I was still on his heels, he said, "Suzanne, this could be dangerous."

"All the more reason I should go with you," I said. "Besides, if you leave me out here all by myself, I may just get jumpy and call the chief myself."

The mayor didn't look happy about my threat, but he wasn't

about to call my bluff, either. Clearly I knew the man better than he thought I did.

"Fine. Stay behind me though, okay? Can you at least do that?"

I nodded, and then I realized that he couldn't see me in the dark. As we headed for the front door, Tori Sheppard stuck her head out of the cottage next door. "What are you two up to? It's the middle of the night."

"Go back to bed, Tori," George said curtly.

It was clear that she was in no mood to be taking his orders. "I'd love to, but some moron just woke me up banging on a pot with a stick."

"Actually, it was a spoon," I said as I held it up toward her, though I doubted that she could see it.

"I don't care if it was your wooden leg," she said. "Just keep it down."

"We'll try our best," I said as I realized that George had suddenly stopped moving just as he'd gotten to the front door.

I was about to ask him why he was hesitating when I glanced down and saw a man's hand and part of his arm sticking out, holding it partially open.

It wasn't moving, and a ball of fear suddenly descended onto me, freezing me in place.

CHAPTER 2

"**I**S IT VAN?" I ASKED George softly. The mayor played the light beam around for a few seconds, and then he turned it back on me. "Yes. From the look of it, he's dead."

"What happened to him?" I asked.

"It appears to me that someone hit him in the back of the head with that," George said as he gestured to a nearby object.

"Is that what I think it is?" I asked as I studied the trophy in the beam of light.

"Yes. It's the April Springs Man of the Year award," he said glumly. I knew that George had just lost the award to Van, and it had been a major point of contention between them. How ironic that someone had used the trophy to kill the councilman. Backing up away from the scene, George pulled out his phone and started dialing.

"Are you calling 9-1-1?" I asked.

"Even better. I'm phoning the police chief on his private line," the mayor said. "Stephen, get over here right now." There was a pause, and then the mayor added, "Sorry. It's early. We're at Van Rayburn's place. Suzanne is with me. Of course I'm talking about Suzanne Hart. Do you know any other Suzannes? What's wrong? No, I haven't been drinking! Van is dead." After another long pause, George said, "I'm pretty sure. Call an ambulance if you want, but if you ask me, the man is beyond all hope. Get over here as soon as you can."

"I'm calling the EMTs, just in case." After he hung up, I reminded George, "We didn't check for a pulse."

"You're looking at the same thing I am," George said softly. "That's a lot of blood. There's no way that he's still alive."

"Still, I'd feel better if we knew for sure," I said as I reached for the flashlight. George gave it up reluctantly, and I approached the body to see if I could find a pulse.

As I leaned down, carefully avoiding the blood, I could swear I saw the man's body twitch! "George, he's still alive!"

"That can't be," the mayor said as I tried to find a pulse at Van's neck.

It was so weak that I nearly missed it, but after a few moments, I caught it, thin and thready. He was still alive, at least for the moment. "What do we do?" I asked in anguish. "We can't just let him die."

The mayor took off his jacket. "We need to stop the blood flow."

"Should we really move him?" I asked. I'd heard horror stories about injuries being inflicted by well-meaning bystanders, and I didn't want to do any more damage to the councilman than someone else had already done.

"We don't have much choice," George said as he leaned forward, preparing to lift Van's head so he could check on the wound.

"Hang on. The ambulance will be here in ten seconds," I said as I heard it ripping toward us.

"Does he really have that long?" George asked me brusquely.

"Stop it!" I ordered, not believing for one second that the mayor would listen to me, but sure enough, he did exactly as I'd requested. The ambulance came screaming up the road toward us, and in no time flat, two paramedics were rushing toward us.

"Did you move him?" one asked us.

"No," I said. "We checked him for a pulse, but that was all."

14

"Good. Step aside," one of them said as he knelt down to check for Van's vital signs. "Mr. Mayor, I need you to move and give us some room to work."

"Come on, George," I said as I tugged at my friend's arm. "Let them do their job."

"Sure. Sorry," the mayor said as he finally got the message and stood. "I can't believe he's still alive. There's so much blood. You know, in all my years as a cop, I never saw someone come so close to bleeding out and still hang on. It figures that Van of all people is too stubborn to die."

I knew George, and I realized that he hadn't meant it to sound the way that it did, but evidently the paramedic didn't know him as well as I did. He glanced at the mayor for a moment before going back to work, but a great deal had been said in that look. The paramedic was clearly thinking that George had been the one to attack Van, though the mayor had been with me the entire time. Or had he? How long could it have been since Van was attacked? Could George have done it and then come to the donut shop immediately afterward, knowing that there was no way the councilman would be joining us?

Stop that, Suzanne, I chided myself. George was my friend, and no matter how much animosity there was between the two men, the mayor would never have attacked the councilman and then left him for dead.

Would other folks believe that, though? I found myself hoping that Van Rayburn managed to hang on for more reasons than just not wanting him to die. If he expired, I had a hunch there would be more than one witness coming forward to testify about the two men's rocky relationship.

"On three," the paramedic who'd stared hard at George said to his partner. With obvious skill and a touch of grace as well, they transferred Van onto their gurney.

As they were loading him into the ambulance, Chief Grant drove up, his lights flashing and his siren screaming.

We were collecting quite a crowd outside despite the early hour. After stopping to speak briefly with the paramedics, the police chief joined us. "Have either one of you been inside the house since you arrived?" he asked us.

"No, we're not idiots," George said. The more stressed he was, the gruffer his demeanor, which was exactly the wrong reaction to the police chief's inquiries.

Chief Grant decided to let that one slide. "Tell me what happened."

"We found his body and called you. Period," George said. "What else do you want to know?"

Stephen Grant shook his head, and I could see him biting his lower lip to keep his own temper in check. I decided that it was time to speak up. "George and Van both won the bids for my donut-making lesson this morning at the silent auction last night. When Van didn't show up, George and I decided to come over here and wake him up."

"What made you think he was still asleep?" the chief asked, clearly groggy from the early hour himself.

"What else would he be doing at three a.m., taking piano lessons?" George asked him.

"How exactly did you find him?" Chief Grant asked as he surveyed the porch with a strong flashlight of his own.

"His hand and part of his arm were outside the front door," I said. "At first we thought he was dead, but then I found a pulse. It was weak, but it was there nonetheless."

The chief glanced at George for confirmation, who protested, "Look at the blood on the porch. What would you think?"

"That I've seen some awfully bad head wounds in my time," he said. "It isn't always necessarily fatal."

The words had been issued gently, but George felt their sting anyway. He was about to say something that I was sure he'd regret when I touched his arm lightly. "Do you need us, Chief, or can we go back to Donut Hearts?" I was well aware of the time factor. With each passing minute, my schedule was getting farther and farther behind, and while I sympathized with Van, I still had donuts to make.

"Give me time to get statements from you," the chief said as two more cruisers pulled up. "I need to check out the interior."

"Can't you come by the shop to get them?" I asked. I was upset about finding Van's injured body, but that didn't mean that I didn't have things I had to do myself in the meantime. It might have seemed heartless to most folks, but I had a job to do, and besides, the attack on Van hadn't had anything to do with me.

"Sorry, but that's going to have to wait." The police chief started inside, and George took a few steps behind him. Chief Grant turned to him and said, "I'm sorry, but you can't go in with me, Mr. Mayor."

"Are you forgetting that I was a cop once upon a time myself?" George asked. "I can handle myself."

"I said no," the chief said firmly.

It was clear that there was no give in his voice, and the mayor nodded in agreement, though he was obviously unhappy about the way Chief Grant was treating him.

One of the chief's men approached us, and he and his boss went inside, being careful to avoid the blood on the front porch.

"Do you think they'll find anyone inside?" I asked George.

"No. Unless I miss my guess, whoever did it is long gone," he said. "I don't know why the chief wouldn't let me go in with him."

"You don't get it, do you?" I asked as I turned and looked at my friend in the headlights from one of the closest squad cars. "George, you *can't* go in there."

"Why not?"

"Because you're going to be everyone's prime suspect," I said, stating the obvious.

The mayor looked shocked by the concept. "I didn't do it!"

"You know that, and I know that, but how is it going to look to most folks? You and Van were just about sworn enemies. You even had a fight last night at the silent auction, for goodness sakes! That's not even mentioning the weapon someone used on him. Do I need to remind you that it was the trophy you claimed was rightfully yours, George?"

Apparently it was finally starting to sink in just how bad things were looking for him. "Suzanne, surely folks around here know me better than to think I'd attack Van, or anyone else, for that matter."

"I don't know. They know me pretty well too, but I've found myself in their crosshairs a time or two over the years," I said. "Mr. Mayor, you need to be very careful right now."

"That's nonsense," he said.

There was nothing more that I could say. "Then go ahead and lose your cool again. It was nice while it lasted."

"What are you talking about?" George asked me.

"Your tenure as mayor," I said.

He took a moment to let that sink in, and as he was still mulling it over, Chief Grant and his officer came back out of the cottage. The chief started shouting orders as soon as he was back outside, and his staff got busy carrying them out.

"Listen, I didn't attack Van," George said the moment the police chief rejoined us.

Chief Grant merely shrugged as he turned to me. "Suzanne, you can go back to Donut Hearts now. I'll come by later to get your statement." Then he looked at George. "Will you be home or in your office?"

"I'll be at Donut Hearts. I'm making donuts with Suzanne," the mayor insisted. "Nothing's changed that."

"Are you telling me that you're going to go ahead and do that *despite* the attack on Van?" the police chief asked him carefully.

"I didn't hit him, so why shouldn't I?" George asked.

"Fine. I'll see you both there soon," he said.

As the mayor and I got back into the Jeep, I reached for my cell phone.

"Who are you calling at this hour, Suzanne?" George asked me.

"Jake," I said. "He'll know what to do."

"I didn't do anything wrong, and I certainly don't need your husband's help to prove it," George said.

"That's where you're wrong," I said as I called Jake.

He answered on the first ring. "I'm on my way," he said the moment he heard my voice. "Are you still at Van's place?"

"No, we're heading over to Donut Hearts," I said. I should have known. Jake often turned on the police-band radio once I left for work every morning. My husband claimed that it soothed him, and I didn't doubt it for one second. After all, he'd been a cop for a very long time before we'd met. "See you in two minutes."

"I'll be waiting for you out front," he said.

As I put my phone away, and before George could say a single word, I told him strongly, "Whatever you're about to say, save it. When we see Jake, you're going to cooperate with him in any way he asks. Do you understand me?"

"Since when did you get so bossy?" George asked me as I drove a little faster than was technically necessary.

"As a matter of fact, I learned it from a good friend of mine. Maybe you know him. He's the mayor," I said.

"Hey, I resent that," George said.

"I'm sorry, did you say that you resemble that?" I asked him with a grin.

He wouldn't budge, though. "You heard me right the first time."

I decided not to answer as we arrived back at Donut Hearts. I parked out front and got out, giving Jake a big hug the moment I saw him. As I did, I whispered in his ear, "Thanks for coming. He's a stubborn old coot, but he needs you."

"No worries," Jake said, and I knew that my friend was in good hands. There was no way that Jake would let George be steamrolled for the attack on the town councilman if he were innocent, which I wanted to believe with all of my heart.

"Would you two like to come inside and talk while I get started on donuts? We have fresh coffee, if you're interested."

"I'm supposed to be helping you make them," George said woodenly.

"Another day, my friend," I said. "For now, you need to talk to my husband."

"I keep telling you that I don't need him," he said, and then he turned to my husband. "No offense, Jake."

"None taken," my husband said amiably. "But you might as well go along with Suzanne's suggestion. We both know that she's going to get her way eventually anyway, so why resist?"

In other circumstances, I might have protested his summation, but in this case, he was absolutely right.

George was going to get my husband's help whether he wanted it or not, and I was going to personally see to it myself.

CHAPTER 3

"**W**OULD YOU TWO MIND? I'M trying to bake in here," I told the two men a little later as I worked in the kitchen.

"Sorry about that. We'll try to keep it down," Jake apologized as he and George sat side by side at the counter out front.

"That's not what I mean. I want you to speak *up*," I clarified. "How else am I going to get anything done and still eavesdrop?"

"Fine. We'll talk louder," Jake replied, suppressing a grin.

As I worked on the cake donut batter for the day, I could hear the two men talking. I wouldn't be able to eavesdrop the entire time they were chatting, but for the moment, I could hear everything they said.

"When was the last time you saw Van?" Jake asked the mayor as he took out one of the small notebooks he always carried with him.

"Do you mean *before* we found him sprawled out on the floor at his house?" George snapped.

Jake didn't blow up. Instead, he said calmly, "George, you can pretend this isn't going to be a problem for you, but we both know that you'd be wrong. If you don't want my help, I completely understand. Shoot, I can even respect it a little, even though we both know that it's the wrong way to approach this, but I won't make a man accept my help."

My husband stood, and I was about to protest when George said, "Hang on a second, Jake. I'm sorry. I know you're just trying to help. I saw Van last night at the auction. That was it. At least until Suzanne and I found him this morning."

"How did you two leave things last night?" Jake asked as he took his seat again.

"It's no secret that we were arguing," George said. I glanced in and saw that the mayor was scowling. "The two of us never got along, and everybody in town knows it. Van has always believed that he would make a better mayor than I ever could, and he wasn't shy about sharing his opinion with anyone who would stop long enough to listen to it. We clashed on just about everything, you know? That doesn't mean that I'm happy that he's been attacked. Who would do something like that?"

"That's what we're going to find out," Jake said.

That managed to perk George up a little. "The two of us?"

"Actually, I was talking about Suzanne and me," he corrected.

"No offense to your wife, but I was a trained law enforcement officer myself, remember? Why does everyone seem to keep forgetting that fact?"

"George, if you go anywhere near this investigation, folks are going to think you're doing it just to try to cover your own tracks," Jake said solemnly. "Suzanne and I are impartial."

"Gee, I sure hope that's not the truth," George said with the hint of a wry smile.

"Of course it's not, but at least neither one of us are suspects," he replied.

"And right now I'm at the top of everyone's list, including the police chief's," the mayor answered.

"Take it easy. Not *everyone's* got you in their crosshairs," Jake said. "I don't think we have to rehash all of the reasons you might have wanted to hurt the man. The real question now is who should we be looking at? Do you have any ideas?"

"If it were me, I'd talk to Buford Wilkins first," George said. "He was in on everything Van did on the council, and as far as

I could see, the two of them were thick as thieves. He's going to be your best source of information."

I saw Jake make an entry in his notebook. "Anybody else?" he asked, his pen still poised over the page.

After a moment or two of thought, the mayor said, "There's his sister, Noreen. She'll probably already be at the hospital by now. Do you know her?"

Jake shook his head, so I piped up from the kitchen, "I've known her for years. Noreen Walker is an acquired taste, if you know what I mean." That was putting it mildly. The woman had a way of antagonizing folks that made Gabby Williams seem downright diplomatic, which was something I would have said was nearly impossible to do in ordinary circumstances.

Jake nodded, and then he turned back to George. "Van makes his living as an insurance agent. Is that right?"

"He's had a *lot* of careers over the years. That's just one of the things he's into at the moment, but rumor is that he has small stakes in at least half a dozen different businesses around the county. Taken individually, you wouldn't think he'd be worth that much, but I suspect the man is loaded."

"Does he have a business partner of any kind?" Jake asked.

"I know that he and Bob Casto have owned a few things together over the years. The two of them had a pretty public blowout a few months ago though, and they haven't spoken since."

"Why didn't I know about that?" I asked from the kitchen. It was nearly time to start dropping cake donuts into the oil, and for once, I was willing to risk leaving the door open so I could hear them talking. The heavy dropper had slipped from my hands once and had indented the wall with the force of its impact, so generally I made Emma leave when I dropped the cake donuts, but I was willing to make an exception this time.

Speaking of my assistant, where was she? By the time I was ready to drop donuts, Emma Blake was usually arriving at work.

"Suzanne, you don't know *everything* that goes on in April Springs," George said with the hint of a laugh in his voice.

"Maybe not, but I know more than most folks do," I said.

"I'm not about to disagree with that," George said.

Jake frowned as he stared at what had to be the meager entries in his notebook. "That covers business and family. Is Van involved with anyone at the moment?"

"Do you mean romantically?" George asked. "I don't have a clue."

"He was seeing Vivian Reynolds, but they had a bad breakup recently," I said as I carefully swung the dropper, forcing the batter down to the bottom where it could be released with the trigger mechanism on top.

"How could you possibly know that?" George asked me.

"Vivian was in here a few days ago. She bought a dozen donuts to go and made some kind of fuss about giving some of her friends my tasty treats, but I could see that she'd been crying, and I pushed her a little about it. It didn't take much of a nudge. She told me that she and Van were through, and that she was giving up on men and devoting herself to charitable works and kind deeds instead. It appeared to me she was going to start by polishing off that entire box of treats by herself, but there wasn't anything I could do about that."

"Do you happen to know who ended the relationship?" Jake asked me.

"He dumped her, and she was pretty bitter about it," I said. "The truth is, that woman has always struck me as being a little nuts."

"Do either one of you have anything else?" Jake asked as he glanced from the mayor to me.

"Not me," I said as I dropped the last few batter rings into the oil.

"That's all I've got," George concurred.

Jake flipped the notebook shut. "All right, then. It should be enough for us to get started."

"How's the chief going to feel about you mucking about in his business?" George asked Jake. "He kind of looks up to you, you know."

"I'll speak with him before I do anything," Jake said. "Besides, he has a soft spot in his heart for Suzanne."

"That's only because I feed him donuts," I said with a laugh.

I heard the front door open.

Emma was there at last.

There was only one problem, though.

She wasn't alone.

"Suzanne, let me state for the record that this wasn't my idea. I told Dad not to come in with me, but he wouldn't listen," Emma said plaintively.

"The people have a right to know what's going on with their mayor," Ray Blake said as I walked out of the kitchen, having pulled out the last cake donut ring from the hot oil.

"Not in my shop they don't," I said as I took Ray's arm and started walking him back to the front door.

"Hang on a second," George said, surprising me. I could see that at least Jake had approved of the eviction, but unfortunately, neither one of us was in charge of the mayor.

"Mr. Mayor, do you wish to make a statement?" Ray asked, his handheld recorder at the ready.

"I wouldn't say a word to him if I were you," Jake told him.

"I second that," I said.

"How is it going to look to your constituents if you refuse to comment on the dire situation?" Ray asked, clearly goading the man into saying something he'd probably regret later.

"For the record, I didn't attack Van Rayburn," George said. "When he wakes up, there's no doubt in my mind that he'll be the first person to clear my good name."

"What makes you think he's ever going to regain consciousness?" Ray asked.

"What makes you say that?" Jake asked him. "What have you heard?"

"Just that it's not looking good," the newspaperman admitted.

"I'm sure you got that information straight from his physician, Ray," I said, knowing that was probably not the case at all.

"As a matter of fact, it was someone on the hospital staff who prefers to remain anonymous," Ray said stiffly.

"Which means it was a custodian or an orderly, and they don't have a clue about what's really going on," Jake said as he stood as well. "Suzanne was right. Ray, you don't have any right to be here."

"Mr. Mayor? Do *you* want me to leave," the newsman asked, "knowing how it's going to look to the fine citizens of April Springs?"

"They'll just have to think what they think. Suzanne and Jake are probably right. You'd better go, Ray," George said with a sigh.

It almost seemed as though the newspaper editor was proud of being thrown out of my donut shop. "On your head let it be," Ray said, and then he walked out.

"I'm so sorry about that, Suzanne," Emma said.

"It's not your fault. I have a pile of dirty dishes waiting for you," I said with a smile. It didn't take Emma long to get the hint.

"I'm on it, boss."

After she was gone, George looked at Jake and then at me. "I'm in trouble, aren't I?"

"It doesn't look good," Jake admitted. "Do you know any good lawyers? You might want one from out of town for this case."

"I have a friend in Newton who's supposed to be pretty good," George said cagily. "Should I call her?"

"It's possible that it could wait until morning," Jake said, "but if it were me, I wouldn't risk it. How well do you know her?"

"Pretty well," George said. "We've been going out for the past two months."

That was a brand-new bombshell I hadn't known about. "Are you kidding? And we're just now hearing about this, George? What's her name?"

"Cassandra Lane," he admitted, "and I didn't want anyone to know. I'm the mayor, but that doesn't entitle everyone to every corner of my private life."

He had a point, so I decided not to berate him about holding out on me. "Understood."

George seemed surprised that I hadn't given him more grief. "Wow, things really must be bad if you're passing up a chance to take a shot at me, Suzanne. I'd better call her right now, despite the hour."

"I'd do that, if I were you," Jake said.

The mayor looked at each of us in turn before he said, "If it's all the same to you two, I'd like to do this in private. In fact, I think I'll head back home before I give her a call. Sorry about the donut lessons, Suzanne."

"They aren't canceled, just postponed," I said, doing my best to buoy his spirits. "We'll have this straightened out in no time."

"I hope you're right," the mayor said, and then he started for the door.

Jake wasn't about to let him go just yet, though. "You need to keep a low profile for the next few days, George."

"I'm not going to cower in my house as though I'm guilty of something I didn't do, if that's what you mean," George protested.

"I'm not suggesting that you do. In fact, you should be in your office at nine a.m. taking care of the day's work as though nothing has happened."

"If I'm doing that, then how am I going to dig into who attacked Van Rayburn?" he asked.

"I told you before. You can't. You're going to have to leave that to Suzanne and me," he said.

"It's going to be hard not getting involved myself," the mayor said.

"Fight the impulse," I said as I kissed his cheek. "We'll talk later. Would you like a few donuts for the road? I can't offer you glazed yet, but I have cake donuts ready."

"Thanks anyway, but I seem to have lost my appetite."

The mayor was more upset than he was letting on if he was passing on some of my donuts. At least he finally realized that he was in trouble and that he needed our help.

"Would you like me to escort you home?" Jake asked him seriously.

George was about to protest when he saw my husband smiling at him. "You almost got me there, Jake."

"Be good, Mr. Mayor," Jake told him.

"I'll try my best, but I can't make any promises," George said.

"I sincerely hope you do more than try," Jake replied.

After he was gone, I looked at Jake. "It's bad, isn't it?"

"Well, it's not good. I suppose it *could* be worse," my husband said with a shrug.

"Short of someone catching George on film swinging that trophy over his head, I don't see how," I said.

"Think again. At least Van's still alive," Jake said sagely.

"That's a fair point. Listen, this can't wait until I close the shop at eleven, can it?"

Jake shrugged. "Things are moving quickly, and if we're going to have any luck, we have to strike fast with our suspects. Don't worry about it, Suzanne. I can solo this morning, and you can join me after you finish up here."

"Sorry, but that's not going to work for me," I said. "Emma, can you come out here for a second?"

She joined us. "I said I was sorry about Dad."

"This isn't about that. Could your mother come by on short notice and help you take over the shop today? Jake and I have things we need to do that can't wait."

"Mom was up when I left," Emma said with a grin. "I know she'd love the distraction."

"Then call her," I said, "and thanks for pitching in."

"You bet," Emma said.

After my assistant went into the kitchen to fetch her phone, I turned to Jake. "See? Problem solved. We can work on this case together all day."

"Is there any chance I can snag a few donuts before we go?" he asked me with a smile. "I left the cottage before I could grab something to eat."

"Of course you can. There has to be *some* advantage to being married to the donut lady."

"I can think of more than just free treats," he said with a smile.

"But they're still a benefit, right?" I asked him, returning his grin with one of my own.

"I never claimed otherwise," he said as his smile broadened even further.

It quickly faded when there was a tap on the front door, though.

Had Ray Blake come back for another stab at us?

No, in some ways, it was worse.

The chief of police was standing outside, and from the expression on his face, he wasn't there to grab a few fresh donuts for himself.

CHAPTER 4

"WHERE'S THE MAYOR?" CHIEF GRANT asked as he looked around the donut shop after I unlocked the front door and let him in.

"He decided to go home," I said, "which is exactly where Jake and I are heading ourselves."

"This is pretty early for you to be leaving the shop, isn't it?" the chief asked as he glanced at his watch.

"What can I say? We have things to do," I said.

"About that," my husband said. "There's something you should know, Chief. Suzanne and I are going to look into what happened to Van Rayburn."

It appeared that my husband was waiting for some kind of blast from our police chief, but instead, Chief Grant simply shrugged. "I kind of figured that you might. You told the mayor that he needed a lawyer, didn't you?" the chief asked Jake softly.

"That sounds ominous. How's Van doing?"

"He's hanging on, but just barely. That's about the best prognosis there is right now. Somebody walloped him pretty hard with that trophy this morning."

"You can't honestly think that the mayor did it, can you?" I asked. I'd been friends with the police chief since he'd been a beat cop, but I'd known George a lot longer.

"It's not part of my job description to jump to conclusions," Chief Grant said, looking much older than his years. The job seemed to take its toll on whoever held it, and I wasn't sure why anyone would even want to be in charge. "I'll leave that to you." Before Jake or I could say anything in our defense, the chief added, "I'm kidding. I get a little sarcastic when I'm beat, and I only got about two hours of sleep last night, if you can call it that."

I felt a sudden flood of sympathy for the man in place of my ire. "Can I get you some coffee, Chief?"

"I probably shouldn't," he said.

"But you will anyway, right?" I asked as I poured him a mug. "Sorry, it's probably a little old. Since I was going to throw it out anyway, you don't have to pay for it." It was a sticking point with our police chief about taking anything for free, but I was telling the truth. I wouldn't have sold it to my customers, so there was no reason that he should have to pay for it.

"How about half price?" he asked.

"Take a sip first, and then we'll negotiate," I told him.

He did as I asked, made a face for a moment, and then he reached into his pocket and pulled out a quarter. "Does that work for you?"

"I think you're being overly generous, but I'll take it," I said with a slight smile, despite the serious nature of his visit.

"You really don't mind if we poke around in this case a little?" Jake asked the chief again.

"Officially? Of course I can't condone that kind of behavior from civilians," he said with a grin.

"How about unofficially?" I asked him.

"I don't like to comment unofficially," he said, "but if I did, I'd suggest that if someone *did* decide to look into who clubbed Van, they keep me informed about their progress. I've got no fingerprints on the weapon, no eyewitnesses, and nothing that might help me figure out what happened until and unless the victim wakes up. I'm not exactly drowning in leads at the moment, so I'm not going to turn down any help that I can get."

"I understand," Jake said with a nod. "If I were still the chief of police, I'd feel the exact same way."

"Believe me, there are times I wish that you were, and I was back to just being Officer Grant," the chief said as he took another sip of my dreadfully stale coffee.

"Come on. Don't be so hard on yourself. You're doing a fine job," Jake said as he put his hand on the chief's shoulder.

"If that were true though, you wouldn't be digging around in this case too, would you?"

It was a fair question, and I had no idea how my husband was going to answer it. Jake took a moment, and then he said, "One of the things I've learned from Suzanne since I retired from the force is that folks will talk more readily to someone out of law enforcement than in it. I'm not claiming that a great many suspects don't identify me immediately as an ex-cop, but I'm learning to soften the edges a little bit at a time. I'm beginning to think that I undervalued the help I got from civilians when I was on the job."

"Was that actually a compliment?" I asked with a smile.

"Suzanne, I compliment you all of the time. Don't act so surprised," Jake said.

"I know that, but what can I say? I never get tired of hearing it."

"So, who's made your suspect list so far?" the chief asked.

"I don't know if you can call them all suspects, but there are some folks we're eager to speak with," I said.

"Do you mind sharing the names with me?" the chief asked.

I glanced at Jake, who nodded his approval. "So far, we know that we want to talk to Buford Wilkins, Vivian Reynolds, Bob Casto, and Noreen Walker," I said.

"I understand Noreen, since she's Van's sister, and I also know that Vivian and Van recently had a bad breakup. It's no secret that Van and his old partner, Bob Casto, didn't get along, but what have you got on Buford? I've heard some chatter about a few minor disagreements between the two men about how to run the town council, but nothing significant, and certainly nothing that would make me believe that Buford could be involved with what happened to Van."

"Oh, we don't have any suspicions about Buford, at least not yet," I admitted, "but George thought he might be a good source of information. I understand the two men were close."

"Maybe not as much as folks around here believe," the chief said. "At least that's the word on the street."

"I've always been curious about something," I said. "Where exactly is this street, and why is everybody there constantly talking about everyone else?"

"Ignore her," Jake said. "She doesn't mind being up at this hour."

"Now I *know* that wasn't a compliment," I said, "so don't try to sell it to me as one."

"I wasn't about to," Jake said with a grin.

I decided to let the jab slide, and I was about to say something else when there was a knock at the door. It was Sharon, Emma's mother and Ray's wife, coming to serve as reinforcements at the donut shop.

As I let her in, I said, "Thanks so much for coming on such short notice."

"I'm happy to do it," Emma's mother said as she avoided making eye contact with either man standing there. "Suzanne, I don't see anyone here but you, and I can't hear a thing. That way when my husband quizzes me later about my time at Donut Hearts, I can tell him the truth."

"I understand," I said, "and I appreciate it, as I'm sure anyone else nearby might be as well, that is if they were here in the first place."

"Speaking hypothetically, they would be most welcome," she said with a smile as she headed back into the kitchen. "Emma, I'm here," Sharon called out to her daughter.

My assistant, now my replacement, at least for the day, poked her head out the door. "Excellent. I have a stack of dirty dishes just waiting for you."

"That's what I like to hear," she said.

After the mother-and-daughter team were busy at work in back, the chief put his mug down. "I'd better be going. I've got a ton of things to do before sunrise."

"That's usually my line," I said.

After I unlocked the front door, Jake and I followed him outside. "Thanks for stopping by."

"All part of the service," he said. "I expect to hear from you two later."

"You can count on it," Jake said as he offered his hand.

After the police chief was gone, I turned to Jake. "Hang on a second. I want to go back inside."

"What's up?"

"You'll see," I said. "I won't be a minute." I walked back inside and made my way into the kitchen. I was really glad that I'd already made the cake donuts. "Do you mind if I grab a few dozen for the road?" I asked Emma as I started folding up boxes to transport them.

"It's your shop," she said with a grin. "Help yourself."

I put together two dozen treats, then I taped the box lids shut. "Thanks. Have a good day, you two."

"You bet," Emma said as her mother nodded, lost in her music. At least I assumed it was music.

"What's she listening to?" I asked.

"She downloaded some Italian lessons onto her iPod," Emma explained. "She's planning her next trip, and she wants to be prepared."

"Have you ever thought about going with her on one of her excursions?" I asked.

"No, that's Mom's thing, not mine. I'd just as soon stay right here, make donuts with you, go to class, and hang out with my boyfriend whenever I have the time. It may seem like a simple life, but I'm happy with it."

"You know what? I think it sounds lovely," I said.

Jake was waiting patiently for me as I emerged from the shop with my boxes. "I thought these might help us."

"They certainly couldn't hurt. Should we head to the hospital now?"

I looked at the clock on my phone. "It's still pretty early. Do I have time to go home and grab a quick shower before we get started? I smell like donuts."

"You don't have to shower for me," my husband said as he took in a deep breath of my scent. "Your donut perfume is wonderful, as far as I'm concerned."

"I appreciate that, but I don't want to attract the wrong crowds," I said with a smile. "After all, you're not the *only* man who likes the scent."

"I don't have any trouble believing that," he said. "Let's go home so you can get ready."

"Would you like a ride?" I asked as I noticed that his truck wasn't in sight.

"Ordinarily I'd walk home, but since you're offering, sure, why not?"

I felt great after taking a shower and throwing on clean clothes. Dawn was barely breaking, but I knew that Noreen was most likely already at the hospital standing vigil for her brother, so we'd be able to talk to her without waiting for a decent hour.

What we did after that would be anyone's guess, but Jake

and I had something to do and someone to interview, and that was enough for the moment.

"Hey, Noreen," I said as we found Van's sister in the emergency room waiting room. I'd stowed one box away in the Jeep and brought the other in with us. "We are both so sorry about Van. How's he doing?"

"So far, there's no change, and no one seems eager to share any word of his condition with me," she said as she eyed the box in my hands.

I flipped open the lid and offered her a donut. "Care for a treat?"

"I don't think I could," Noreen replied. Her eyes were red, and the balled-up tissues in her hands told me that she'd been crying.

"Go on. You need to eat something," I said. Ordinarily I didn't like pushing my treats on people, but I thought she could use a boost.

"Well, maybe just a bite," she said as she picked out a sour cream donut.

"That's one of my favorites, too," I said. "I'm sorry we didn't bring any coffee."

"I'll go grab some," Jake said. He nodded slightly to me, giving me his approval to continue my questioning without him. Noreen had stiffened the moment she'd realized that Jake was with me, and she hadn't been able to keep from glancing at him since we'd first arrived. My husband had that effect on some people. It was nearly impossible disguising the fact that he'd been a cop for a very long time, and a great many folks were uncomfortable talking around him, no matter how disarming he tried to be. He was working on it, but he still had a way to go. As for me, I was a simple donut maker in most people's eyes, and I liked it that way. It made it much easier for them to talk to me, and I tried my best to take full advantage of that fact.

After Jake was gone, I said softly, "You must be terrified about your brother's situation." We were in the emergency room waiting area, and there must have been some kind of crash earlier, based on the people milling about so early in the morning and their conversations. It was hard to get the space to speak with Noreen without other folks listening in, but then I realized that none of them were concerned about us at all. They had their own problems to deal with, and as far as they were concerned, Noreen and I weren't even there.

"I am worried sick about him," she said, balling up the tissues in one hand harder and harder. I had great concern for the donut I'd given her based on the rigid way she was holding it as well.

"Do you have any idea who might have done such a thing?" I asked her as sympathetically as I could manage.

"I do, but you're not going to like it, since he's a friend of yours," she said icily.

"I can assure you, no matter what you might think, George didn't do this to Van," I said, automatically defending my friend, no matter what it might cost me in my investigation.

"But then again, you *have* to say that, don't you?" Noreen asked. She was around my mother's age, but the years hadn't been nearly as kind to her as they had been to Momma. Angry wrinkles showed on her face and hands, and her clothes had been in style a few seasons earlier. I also noticed that her shoes were well worn, and there was a safety pin in the hem of her dress. Noreen tried her best to look prosperous, but it was clear that it was in appearance only, merely a façade of what was really going on with her. That made me wonder about something. Was she her brother's lone heir? If she was, I had an uneasy feeling that her motive might be the strongest one of all the people in Van's life. Was she there as his concerned sister, afraid that he would never wake up, or was it more sinister than that? Was she actually afraid that he would regain consciousness soon and be able to name her as his attacker?

"Suzanne? What are you thinking about?"

I'd stayed silent for so long that I'd aroused her suspicions, something I couldn't afford to do if I was going to get her to confide in me. "I was just thinking about the last time I saw your brother," I lied. "It was at the silent auction. He was so interested in learning about how donuts were made. I'm upset that someone robbed him of the experience. When did *you* see him last?"

"I wasn't at the auction," she replied. "We had lunch yesterday, though." Her words faltered a little as she said it, and I had to wonder if something tense had occurred during their meal.

"Did something happen between you?" I asked. After all, why not go straight to the source for my answer?

"No, not really," she said, dismissing my question. "Suzanne, I can't talk about it, okay? I'm so worried about my brother."

"Have they told you *anything*?" I asked her.

"Just that the next twenty-four hours are critical," she said.

"Would it help talking about who else might have done this?" I asked her. "It might take your mind off Van's condition."

Noreen looked as though she were about to cry again, but she found a way to fight it back. With a look of disgust on her face, she said, "Bob Casto has to be near the top of my list. Those two fought like junkyard dogs not two weeks ago." It was the first hint of the bitter woman I'd known all along. The only thing that had surprised me was how long it had taken that side of her to come out.

"What about Vivian Reynolds?" I asked.

"That tramp? What about her? My brother dumped her for good reason. If she dares to show her face around here, she'll soon wish that she hadn't," Noreen said angrily. For Vivian's sake, I hoped that she stayed away. The last thing anyone needed was the two of them going at it in the ER waiting room.

I was about to ask her if there was anyone else we should know about when Buford Wilkins came in. Noreen stood and rushed into his arms as though they were lifelong friends, and I had to wonder about their relationship as their embrace lingered long past when it would have been acceptable to break. Was there something more than friendship going on between the two of them? Though Buford was a short and heavyset man with very little hair, he acted as though he thought he was God's gift to women. I couldn't help noticing as he sat down beside her that her hands naturally clutched at his.

"How is Van doing? Forgive me, but I just heard about what happened."

"The doctors are all saying that it's too soon to tell," she said.

"Is he awake yet?" Buford asked eagerly.

"No, at least not as far as I know. They haven't told me anything new for hours, though."

"We'll just see about that," Buford said as he stood. On his way to the front desk, it seemed as though he noticed me for the first time. "What are you doing here, Suzanne?"

His reaction was a little defensive for my taste. "I thought Noreen should eat something while she was waiting to hear about her brother." I offered the box to him. "Care for a donut?"

"No," he said flatly, and then he must have realized how abrupt he'd sounded. "You know what? I changed my mind. Is the offer still open?"

"Sure, why not?" I asked, not really wanting to refuse him. After all, my donuts had paved the way for me before when I was questioning folks, and I had high hopes that they would work their magic yet again.

Buford grabbed the nearest chocolate glazed donut and took

a single bite that nearly demolished the entire thing. "Got any coffee?" he asked as crumbs fell out of his mouth.

It was all I could do not to take a few steps back to get out of the way.

"Did someone say coffee?" Jake asked as he showed up with a tray holding three cups. "I can't make any promises, since Barton's not on duty yet." As the executive chef of the hospital's cafeteria, Barton Gleason provided food that was quite a bit above what most folks expected from such fare.

"Thanks," Buford said as he grabbed two cups, taking one for himself and handing the other to Noreen.

Jake looked at me, and all I could do was shrug. We'd get more coffee later. At the moment, this interview was more important.

Only we weren't going to get to have it quite yet.

I saw Noreen suddenly stiffen, and when I looked in the direction she was glaring, I watched as Vivian Reynolds walked in, looking as though she was there to pick a fight.

And I had a hunch she was about to get exactly that.

CHAPTER 5

"WHAT ARE *YOU* DOING HERE?" Noreen snarled as she got out of her seat in a flash.

"That's no concern of yours. I have every right to be here," Vivian snapped back, clearly unafraid of Van's sister. She was an attractive woman in a brassy sort of way, and it didn't surprise me that a great many men found her attractive, though her personality was a little too volatile for my taste. "This hospital is public property."

"Van doesn't need you anywhere near him. You already came close to killing him before. What are you doing here? Are you coming back to finish what you started?"

Vivian looked as though she'd been physically struck by the words. "I never laid a hand on him," she protested loudly, making absolutely certain that everyone around heard.

"Maybe not physically, but you broke his heart," Noreen said.

"In case you need reminding, *he's* the one who broke up with *me*," Vivian countered.

"Because you cheated on him!" Noreen yelled. We were collecting quite a crowd, and I had to fight my instincts to break the two women up. It wasn't pretty by any means, but if both of them were highly agitated, maybe they'd let something important slip out. It wasn't the most compassionate thing I'd ever done in my life, but we needed all the help we could get figuring out what had really happened to Van Rayburn.

George's very freedom might depend on it.

"I did no such thing!" Vivian screamed. "It was all in your brother's mind!"

I may not have been willing to separate them, but clearly Buford had no such compunction. The man was braver than I would have ever given him credit for as he stepped between the two angry women, putting himself directly in harm's way. "Ladies, you both need to take a deep breath and settle down."

"She needs to leave!" Noreen snapped.

"You first," Vivian countered.

"If you don't back off, and I mean right now, you're both about to be thrown out of here," Buford said as he pointed to an approaching security guard.

It was time to act. I grabbed Vivian's arm and said, "Let's go outside and take a deep breath of fresh air. What do you say?"

"I don't have to go anywhere," she said reluctantly.

"Would a donut help?" I asked, reaching for the box.

Buford looked troubled by my maneuver. Had he honestly thought they were all for him? If he had, he was sadly mistaken.

"I don't know. Maybe," she said reluctantly. "But I'm not leaving for good," she snapped over her shoulder at Noreen.

"That's what you think," Noreen said, returning fire.

"We'll be right back," I told Jake. I didn't want to leave Noreen and Buford alone, and besides, I had a hunch that Vivian might speak with me a little easier if he weren't around. Jake took it in stride, staying behind while I walked Vivian out the door.

Once we were outside, I offered her a donut. She looked over the remaining selection, and then she shook her head. "I changed my mind. No offense, but I don't want one."

I tried not to take the rejection personally. "You don't have to eat one, then," I said. "What was Noreen talking about in there?"

"The woman lives in a world full of her own delusions. She has a way of getting under my skin that drives me crazy."

Along with the rest of April Springs, I said to myself. "Was Van right, though?"

"About me cheating on him? No way. I thought we had something good, and then he dumped me for somebody else. It was an excuse, plain and simple, only I wasn't going to take it. I was going to win him back, no matter the cost, but now this happens, and I might lose him forever."

Her determination was a little frightening in its intensity. "Do you know who he was seeing?"

"You'd better believe it! I caught them together!"

"Who was it?" I asked.

"Gabby Williams. What a tramp."

I had heard Gabby referred to by a dozen different names over the years, but "tramp" had never been one of them. So that was why she'd fought so hard to win Grace's makeover at the silent auction. She'd been trying to impress Van. "What does Gabby have to say about it?" I asked, having a hard time thinking of my friend as some kind of temptress.

"She claimed that Van pursued her while he was dating me, but she didn't know that we were still together. The joke was on her, though. Van was breaking up with her last night if he ever got the chance so he could get back together with me," Vivian said triumphantly.

"Did Gabby know that?" I asked, wondering if Vivian had just given my friend a motive for murder.

"How should I know? Van said he was going to tell her after the auction last night. Ask him when he wakes up. Don't ask Gabby, though. She'll probably just lie about it."

"*If* he wakes up," I said, not thinking about how it must have sounded.

For just a moment, Vivian's façade cracked a little. "Is it really that bad?"

"When George and I found him, it didn't look good," I admitted.

"I can't lose him," Vivian said, grabbing my arm so hard that it hurt. "I won't."

"I'm afraid now all we can do is wait," I said. "Vivian, do you have any idea who might have attacked him?"

She looked exasperated by my question. "It could be *anyone*. Van made his share of enemies around town, including your good friend, George Morris."

"The mayor claims that he's innocent," I said.

"What else *would* he say?" she asked me pointedly. "You don't think he's actually going to *confess* to the attack, do you?"

"When was the last time you saw Van?" I asked, trying to get her focus off my friend.

"During the silent auction," she admitted. "We were talking about our plans to get back together when Buford called him on his cell phone."

"What was the call about?"

"Who knows? It was probably just another made-up emergency to do with the town council. Buford thinks of himself as Van's right hand, and he's always stirring something up, as if Van doesn't have enough on his plate dealing with the mayor."

"What about Bob Casto?" I asked her.

"What about him?" Vivian asked in return.

"How bad were things between the two of them?"

"Well, Bob was getting ready to sue Van, if that tells you anything," Vivian said.

"Sue him? Over what?"

"What do you think? Bob did some sneaky things behind

Jessica Beck

Van's back over the years, and when Van found out about them, he was furious. There was a payment that Van controlled, and Bob was supposed to get half of it. Van held up the money until he could get a proper account of what Bob had been up to toward the end of their partnership, so Casto decided to take him to court, if you can believe that!"

Jake came out at that moment, motioning frantically to me. I wasn't nearly finished with Vivian yet, but it looked urgent. "Hang on. I'll be right back," I said.

"What's going on?" I asked Jake.

"It's Van. Apparently he's awake."

Vivian overheard our conversation. "He's awake? I have to see him!" she shouted as she brushed past us and headed inside.

"Sorry about that, Suzanne, but I thought you'd want to know," Jake said.

"You did the right thing," I replied.

As we moved back inside, Jake asked me softly, "Did you learn anything new?"

"A bunch," I said. "Apparently Van was dating Gabby Williams, but he was planning on breaking up with her last night to be with Vivian again."

Jake whistled softly. "It would take a man braver than me to break up with that woman. She must have been furious."

I didn't like the way that was starting to sound. "Remember, we have only Vivian's word that was the case."

"I understand, but we still have to pursue it."

"Of course. Also, apparently Bob Casto was cheating Van toward the end of their partnership, but Bob was the one suing Van for nonpayment of assets he felt belonged to him."

"Wow, Van has a real knack for making enemies, doesn't he?" Jake asked.

"More than I ever imagined. I don't like it, but we're going to need to speak with Gabby about this."

"I agree, but let's see what's going on with Van first," Jake said. "Our entire investigation might be moot if he can identify his attacker."

We hurried toward Van's room, where he'd evidently been transferred while I'd been talking to Vivian. From what Jake told me, the orderly had banged his bed on a wall during the move, and it had been enough to bring Van out of his unconscious state. I wondered if the technique was something they would start trying with other patients.

We couldn't get in. That privilege was reserved for Noreen, and Noreen only, as his only close kin. As we all waited outside, there was a tenseness in the air that only multiplied when Chief Grant came hurrying in. "I just got the call. Where is he?"

I pointed to Van's room, and Chief Grant nodded his thanks as he barged straight in. I heard Noreen protest, but it was quickly silenced. The chief was getting that air of command about him that didn't allow dissent.

I heard more voices inside, and then Noreen came out, her face red with anger. "They threw me out. Can you believe it?"

"Is it true? Is Van really awake?" I asked her.

"He's groggy, and he doesn't remember much about the last twenty-four hours, but yes, he's awake, no thanks to whoever tried to kill him." She said that last bit glaring at Vivian, who, for once, refused to rise to the bait.

"Then it's just a matter of time before he names his attacker," I said.

That caused several odd looks among those waiting for news. Why weren't they all happier about that fact? Could it be that one of them had been the one wielding the trophy, and they were about to be named by the victim?

Jessica Beck

Ten minutes later, the chief came out alone. He turned to Noreen as he said, "You can go back in."

"It's about time," she said abruptly as she brushed past him.

"You're only going to be able to stay for a few minutes," Chief Grant told her. "He needs his rest."

"What did he say to you?" Noreen asked as she pivoted and glared at him. "Did he name his attacker?"

"Just go see your brother," the chief said with a sigh.

Noreen frowned, but ultimately, she did as she was told.

After she was gone, the rest of us surrounded the police chief. "What did he say? Who did it? Is it finally over? Are you going to arrest someone for the attack?" He was pelted with questions, but he clearly wasn't in the mood to supply any answers.

"Folks, I'm sorry to refuse you all, but I'm not about to answer questions in the middle of an ongoing investigation."

No one liked it, but there was really nothing any of us could do about it. As the chief started to go, Jake said, "Hold up a second, Chief." As my husband caught up with his one-time protégé, he shot me a look that told me that this time, *I* was the one who wasn't welcome to the party. Fair enough. He was right. There would be a much better chance that the chief would speak with him if I didn't tag along, and after all, turnabout was only fair play.

While I waited for Jake and the chief to have their conversation, I turned back to Buford, who was scowling as he busily typed away on his phone. "Trouble?" I asked him.

"Not really. I suspect that the mayor is going to try to push something through with Van laid up, but I'm not about to let that happen."

"I doubt that's true," I said. I couldn't imagine George taking advantage of the situation like that.

"Well, doubt all you want to, but it's what Van or I would

48

do if the roles were reversed, and I'm going to be ready, just in case."

"You don't much care for George, do you?" I asked. "Are you still smarting about losing the election to him?" George had defeated Buford pretty soundly in the most recent general election, though Buford had at least retained his seat on the council.

"It's all politics," Buford said with a shrug. "You win some, and you lose some."

"You're still third in line for the throne though, aren't you?" I asked.

Buford looked at me with a scowl. "What are you talking about?"

"I remember my April Springs civics lessons from high school," I said. "We don't have an assistant mayor around here. If George can't serve, then Van takes his place. If Van can't, you're next in line based on seniority, aren't you?"

"It's not going to come to that," Buford said dismissively. "Besides, who in their right mind would even *want* that job? It's gotten George Morris nothing but grief since he first took office. I was nuts to run myself, and you can take my word for it, it's never going to happen again."

At that point, Buford's cell phone rang. After glancing at the caller ID, he said, "Sorry. I have to take this call."

As Buford held a whispered consultation with whoever was on the other end of the line, I had to wonder why anyone would take the small-town political infighting so seriously when a man's life had so recently been at risk?

Jake came back and motioned toward me. "Feel like taking a drive, Suzanne?" he asked me.

"Should we really just leave when Van is finally awake? Did the chief say who might have attacked him?"

"Noreen wasn't lying when she said that Van couldn't

remember a thing about the assault. The doctor told Chief Grant that it was some kind of amnesia, probably temporary, and that most likely, he'll recall it sooner or later."

"That makes him a danger to his attacker, doesn't it?" I asked, concerned that whoever had hit the councilman might try to come back and finish the job.

"I told the chief the same thing. He's going to post one of his men as a guard in front of Van's door, at least as long as he's in the hospital. In the meantime, we need to continue with our investigation. Do you feel like paying Bob Casto a visit?"

"That sounds good to me," I said as we headed for my Jeep. I was glad that we had another dozen donuts stashed away there. It would probably take at least that many treats to get Bob to speak with us. As I drove, I asked Jake, "How did you get the police chief to tell you all of that?"

Jake shrugged. "I had to tell him everything we'd uncovered so far first, including Gabby's possible involvement in the case. Sorry about that, but it was the only way he'd give up what was going on with Van."

"Gabby's a big girl," I said, "but maybe we should give her a heads up before we go off in search of Bob Casto."

"Sounds good to me," Jake said. "Would you like some company when you talk to her?" he added, clearly reluctant to even make the suggestion.

I had to laugh. "Thanks, but we both know that's a hollow offer. She's not going to want to talk to me about her love life, let alone include you in the conversation."

"Then I'll make myself scarce while you two chat," Jake said with a gentle smile.

"I appreciate it, but don't wander off too far. I might need backup if things get ugly."

"Suzanne, how can you possibly believe that it will be anything other than ugly?"

"You're right, but let me have the fantasy at least as long as it takes me to drive to ReNEWed, okay?"

"Okay," Jake agreed.

As I drove the few short miles to Gabby's store, I realized that by the time we got there, she'd be opening her doors to the public. I couldn't even use the time of day as an excuse.

Like it or not, Gabby Williams and I were about to have a very uncomfortable conversation that neither one of us was going to enjoy.

CHAPTER 6

"I'M NOT OPEN YET," GABBY called out with her back to me as I walked into ReNEWed. Even though her inventory was gently used, most of the clothes Gabby carried were out of my league, though I'd bought things from time to time from her in the past.

"That's fine, because I'm not here to shop," I told her as a store mannequin glared down at me. It was almost as though the dummy knew that the clothes on its back were well beyond my budget.

"Hello, Suzanne," Gabby said as she turned to face me. She'd clearly been crying, and unfortunately, I was most likely about to make it worse.

"I'm so sorry about Van," I said, trying to muster every bit of sympathy I could for my friend. I'd been reluctant to call her that not that long ago, but I'd realized lately that we were indeed friends, no matter how odd that fact struck me most of the time.

"Did he die?" Gabby asked, sobbing openly now. "I never even had the chance to say good-bye to him."

"No. He's not dead. In fact, he woke up less than an hour ago," I explained.

Gabby's tears turned into fury, which was now directed straight at me. "Suzanne, I don't know what kind of sick game you're playing, but I don't appreciate it."

"I'm not playing any games at all," I explained quickly. I'd wanted to be smoother about bringing up her recently ended relationship with Van, but that ship had clearly sailed. "I heard that you two were dating, so I knew you'd be upset about what happened to him."

"Who told you about that?" Gabby asked me, the fire still burning brightly in her stare.

"Does it matter? It's true, isn't it? I also heard that he dumped you last night," I said, blurting out the words without even giving them too much thought. If I weighed and considered every word that I said to Gabby, I knew that I'd lose my nerve, and I needed to know what was going on, even if it riled her up a little.

Or a lot, as the case might be.

"He would never dump me!" she exclaimed. "We are in love."

"Really? How long have you two been going out?" I asked her.

"Time doesn't matter when you know it's right," she said just a tad too defensively for my taste. Anyone else, at least anyone with the slightest bit of common sense, would have dropped it right there.

Unfortunately, I wasn't in any position to do that.

"Gabby, enough with the histrionics. I need to know what happened. I'm sorry to be so blunt, but I have to know what's going on. You want Jake and me to find his attacker, don't you?"

"Of course I do," Gabby said meekly. "I really should go to him." There wasn't a great deal of conviction in her voice, and I suspected that they had split up indeed, despite her earlier denial.

"Why don't we have a little chat first?" I asked. "Noreen is guarding his hospital room door pretty closely, so I'm not sure you'd be able to get in even if you tried to pay him a visit."

"I suppose Vivian is there as well," Gabby said, the darkness in her expression deepening.

"She's not standing by the door, if that's what you're asking. As a matter of fact, Noreen tried to run her out of the building."

Gabby smiled at that, if only for a moment. "I would expect

nothing less of her. Suzanne, tell me the truth. Is he going to recover?"

"They don't know yet. The thing is, he doesn't remember who attacked him, so Jake and I are digging into what happened."

"What do you mean, he doesn't know? Just how badly is he hurt?" Gabby looked genuinely concerned at hearing the news.

"I have no idea. The fact that he's awake and talking at all is a miracle as far as I'm concerned," I said, flashing back to finding Van sprawled out through the front door, his arm lying there lifeless as though he were already dead. "I need to know the truth, Gabby, no matter how painful it might be for you to tell it."

"Fine," she finally said softly. "It's true; all of it. We were dating, but last night at his place, he said that he wasn't sure who he belonged with, Vivian or me. He said he needed time, and ultimately, I agreed to give it to him."

"Did you two argue about it?" I asked, knowing Gabby well enough to realize that she wouldn't go down without a fight.

"We had words," she admitted, "but I never laid a hand on him, and I certainly didn't hit him with that trophy. I'm the one who made that happen in the first place, you know," she said a little proudly.

"What are you talking about?"

"George was a certainty to get the award, but I'm on the committee that names the winner, and I used my influence to secure the victory for Van," she admitted.

I had to wonder if that had been the entire reason Van Rayburn had been dating her. I knew that he loved nothing more in the world than sticking it to George, and that must have been the ultimate prize, at least in his mind. It was a wonder that Van hadn't awakened from his coma and named George his attacker, whether it were true or not. In fact, if the councilman had been thinking clearly, I was willing to bet that he would have done just that.

"Was it that important to you to make him happy?" I asked Gabby, knowing that her principles were something she thought highly of.

"Suzanne, you don't understand. You're young and pretty, and you've got Jake. Who do I have?"

"Gabby, I'm sure there's someone out there for you, too," I said.

"Don't patronize me," she said, her momentary softness gone. "I know better than anyone that my chances of finding love again are slipping away with each passing moment. I fully realize that I shouldn't have done what I did, but I'm not at all sure that I wouldn't do it all again if I were given the opportunity. George doesn't need any more accolades. He's already the mayor, for goodness sake. Losing that award didn't hurt him any, and it was so important to Van."

Gabby could stand there justifying her actions all morning long, but that didn't mean that I had to listen to them. "Do you have any idea who might have attacked Van? And don't say George. I won't tolerate that."

Gabby looked surprised by the implication. "The truth is, George Morris never crossed my mind as a suspect."

"I'm glad you think so well of him," I said, surprised by her momentary kindness.

"Oh, he's capable of murder, but I doubt that he'd hit anyone from behind. If the attacker had run Van down with their car or shot him in the face, I would have begged the police chief to talk to the mayor first."

I didn't agree with her assessment of my friend's potential homicidal tendencies, but I wasn't about to get into that, either. "Do you have a list of suspects in your mind?"

"Well, Noreen has to be at the very top," Gabby said.

"Why is that?" I'd suspected that the woman was in need of money, but I was curious to hear what Gabby had to say.

"Suzanne, she's stone cold broke, and when and if Van dies, she gets every last dime of his estate. At least that's what she thinks. She's going to be in for a surprise if that happens, though."

"Why would she be surprised?"

"Good old Van is broke himself. He puts on a good front, but I'd hate to tell you how many things I had to pay for while we were dating."

"Funny, but I was under the impression that he had money," I said.

"He did at one time, but he's really not that good a businessman, and he squandered it all away. I know Bob Casto is suing him over a broken deal, but even if he wins, it's going to be a moral victory in name only."

"Does Noreen have any idea that Van is broke?" I asked.

"Oh, no. Van thought it was funny to make his sister think he was rich. You should have seen the way she salivated whenever he talked about leaving everything to her in his will."

If that were true, it would certainly give Noreen motive enough to want to see her brother out of the picture. "Is there anyone or anything else we should consider?" I asked her.

"No one I'm sure you haven't thought about yourself already," Gabby said, but then she frowned for a moment.

"What's wrong?"

"Forget it. It's probably nothing," she said.

"Tell me anyway," I encouraged her.

"After I left Van the first time last night, I drove around town for half an hour thinking about what he said. I decided that I wasn't going to just accept it, so I went back to his place to argue my case further. There was a problem when I got there, though."

"What was it? Was he already gone?" I asked.

"No, but someone else was clearly there. Van was circumspect about it, but he wouldn't open the door all the way, and he certainly wasn't about to let me inside."

"Could it have just been your imagination?" I asked her. "After all, you were understandably upset."

"I heard someone bump into a table in the other room, and Van doesn't have any pets. You do the math, Suzanne."

So, someone had paid the councilman a visit after Gabby had left for the first time. Could it have been his ultimate attacker, or had it been more innocent than that?

"Okay, I believe you. But you two weren't dating at that point. He had the right to see whoever he chose to."

"Not when he had to know in his heart that he truly belonged with me," Gabby said, and then she slapped her hand down on the counter. "Do you know what? Even with his flaws, and believe me, they are many, I still love that man, and I'm not going to let Noreen or anyone else keep me from seeing him."

"What about your shop?" I asked her. "You can't just shut the place down ten minutes after opening for the day."

"Oh no? Just watch me," she said as she slapped a CLOSED sign up in the window. "Come on, Suzanne. I need to get out of here."

"Do you want me to go with you?" I asked, hoping she didn't agree. I didn't want to leave Jake alone to investigate, but then again, it wasn't fair to let Gabby face Noreen, and possibly Vivian as well, all by herself.

"It's sweet of you to offer, but I need to do this on my own," she said.

We left the store together, and after Gabby locked up, she turned back to me and gave me a surprising hug. "Thanks for the pep talk, Suzanne."

"It's funny, but I don't remember giving you one," I said sincerely.

Gabby just chuckled. "Always the kidder, aren't you?"

After she was gone, Jake joined me on the sidewalk in front of the gently used clothing shop. "What was that all about?"

"I have no idea," I said, "but I'll catch you up to speed on our way to Bob Casto's place."

"Sounds good," Jake said, and once again, we were off.

The only problem was that Bob wasn't there.

We were standing outside his office trying to figure out if he was coming in for the day or if he was playing hooky when a man from next door came out. It was Mattie Jones, an infrequent customer at Donut Hearts.

"Are you two looking for Bob?" he asked the moment he saw us. I'd collected the last box of donuts from the back of the Jeep, and I had it tucked under one arm.

"We are. Is he coming in today?" I asked.

"I don't see how that's humanly possible. Haven't you heard?"

"Heard what?" Jake asked.

"Bob had himself an accident this morning. Around two a.m., he wrapped his truck around a telephone pole."

I hadn't paid any attention to the other folks in the emergency room when we'd been there earlier. If I had, I might have realized that they were relatives of the man we were looking for right now.

"Is he okay?" I asked Mattie.

"Not so much. He's banged up pretty good, from what I've heard. He's certainly not in any shape to eat donuts," he added with a grin. "Got one to spare?"

"Sure. Why not?" I asked as I lifted the lid and let him choose one.

After he grabbed a chocolate iced cake donut, he said, "See you."

"Thanks for coming out," I said.

"For a free donut, anytime! It was my pleasure."

After Mattie was gone, I turned to look at Jake, who was scowling. "What's wrong?" I asked him.

"Suzanne, doesn't it seem to you as though it's a mighty big fluke that two former business partners end up in the emergency room within a few hours of each other?"

"I know you don't like coincidences, but they do happen sometimes in real life," I said as we headed back to the Jeep. "We need to go back to the hospital to see how Bob's doing."

"I'd certainly like to ask him a few questions," Jake said.

"Such as?" I asked as I drove us back to the hospital yet again that morning.

"Well, I'd love to know where he was going in so much of a hurry in the middle of the night that he wrecked his truck," Jake said.

"What are you thinking? I'm guessing that you already have a theory about that."

"Let's say for one second that Bob is the one who beat Van with that trophy. What would he do if he thought he might have killed his former partner? A lot of men would want to get away as quickly as they could. We know Van was attacked sometime between eleven and three, which is within the time frame when Bob had his wreck. Is it so hard to believe that he trashed his truck fleeing the scene of the crime?"

"It's not hard to believe at all," I said with a frown. "Could it really be that simple?"

"Sometimes things are exactly as they appear to be. Maybe we should tell the chief about our theory."

"You're right. You should call him," I said as I continued driving.

"It wouldn't hurt, would it? I'll put the call on speaker so you can take part in the conversation, too."

"Thanks. I'd appreciate that."

Jake dialed the number, and Chief Grant picked up almost

instantly. "Chief, this is Jake and Suzanne. Did you hear about Bob Casto?"

"Sure, one of my deputies is out there now measuring the skid marks at the scene," the chief said. "Why do you ask?"

"We thought it might have something to do with the attack on Van," Jake said.

"I considered it," the chief said, "but unfortunately, Bob is so hopped up on painkillers he's not saying anything that makes any sense at all at the moment. I tried questioning him, but it's going to be at least six hours before I can get anything out of him, if then."

"Is Van still awake?" I asked.

"Yes, not that he's been able to tell me much about what happened. The last few days are a real fog for him. In fact, he didn't even remember breaking up with Gabby Williams. Did you know about that?"

"I didn't realize that he'd forgotten about it," I said, hedging my bets.

"But you knew that they were dating and that he dumped her last night?" the chief asked, pushing me a little harder.

"I just found out myself. We were going to tell you about it after we discussed Bob's situation," I said. I hadn't been planning to rat Gabby out so quickly, but then again, there was no telling if I would have told the chief about it without prompting or not if he hadn't brought it up first. "How did you find out about it?"

"Gabby stormed into Van's room two minutes ago claiming that she wasn't accepting his breakup and demanding another chance. Noreen started yelling at her, and then Vivian stuck her nose into it. I had to throw all three of them out. I swear to you, Van thanked me after they were gone. When he recovers, he's going to have a real mess on his hands."

"I have a feeling that he'll be happy if that's his worst

problem," Jake said. "Have you made any progress since we spoke?"

"No, but I'm grinding away at it. The neighborhood canvass didn't turn up anything, and unfortunately, there aren't any security cameras near Van's place. I'm pushing and pulling in a few places, but so far, I'm not having much luck."

"Join the club," Jake said wryly.

"Sure, but no one's counting on you to solve this. I'm hoping that Van recovers his memory sooner rather than later," the chief said.

"If you need someone to help guard his room in the meantime, I'm willing to volunteer my services," Jake said. "I know your overtime budget is tight right now."

"How could you possibly know that? Have you been talking to the mayor?" Chief Grant asked with a sigh.

"No, I overheard it by accident between two of your men the other day," Jake replied.

"I wish they weren't all so chatty," the chief said. "Did you ever have to deal with that when you had my job?"

"Only every day," Jake said with a laugh. "Do you mind if we take a run at Bob Casto? We're nearly at the hospital now anyway."

"Be my guest," he said. "Just don't forget to share, though I doubt you're going to learn anything from him anytime soon."

"Thanks. We'll touch base later."

Jake hung up, and then he turned to me as I parked in the visitor's lot. "Suzanne, after what the chief just told us, is there even any use going in?"

"What can it hurt? Besides, it's getting close to lunchtime, and since we're already here, maybe we can catch a bite to eat in the cafeteria."

"Sounds good to me," Jake said as we got out. "Should I bring the donuts?"

"You might as well," I said. "They won't be good much longer anyway."

"That's a matter of opinion," Jake said.

"Not really, but it's sweet that you say so," I replied.

CHAPTER 7

A S PROMISED, FROM THE SOUNDS coming from his hospital room, Bob was nearly incoherent, so we decided to postpone our visit until after lunch. Jake was ready to give up and head straight for the cafeteria, and since there was no one else around we could interrogate, I agreed.

"I wonder what's on the menu today?" I asked. "Something exotic, maybe."

"I sincerely doubt it. Barton probably can't get too creative with the menu, especially at lunch," Jake said. "If I were you, I wouldn't get my hopes up."

"What fun is that?" I asked him playfully.

We grabbed two trays and got in line, waiting to be served. Since Barton Gleason had taken over, folks from all across our part of the state came to the hospital cafeteria to eat, and who could blame them? I felt a little guilty abandoning Trish at the Boxcar Grill for our noonday meal, but since we were already there, it wasn't that hard to convince myself that we were doing it for logistics and not for taste. I ended up with a large bowl of barbeque macaroni and cheese, a plate of fried pickles, and some coleslaw that tasted better than any I'd ever had in my life, including my mother's recipe.

"That's a really healthy selection you've got yourself there," Jake said with a grin. He'd opted for tomato soup and grilled cheese, though I knew the soup had a dozen levels of flavor and the cheese was a blended mix that was amazing, served on bread that Barton had made fresh that morning himself.

"Hey, there's cabbage in the slaw, and carrots, too, and the pickles were cucumbers once upon a time. This is all practically health food."

"If you say so," Jake said skeptically.

"Who cares, though? It's delicious. I know that much. In fact, yours looks pretty good, too."

"If it tastes anywhere near as good as it smells, I'm sure that it will be," he said.

I was beginning to regret not my choices but the lack of space on my tray. "Tell you what. I'll share some of mine with you if you'll share some of yours with me," I said with a grin.

"It's a deal," he answered happily.

As we ate, delighting in each bite, I noticed a group of folks I'd seen earlier gathered off to one side of the cafeteria. I still had my box of donuts, at least most of them, so I decided to approach them as soon as Jake and I finished our meals. Once we were done, too quickly for my taste, I said, "If you'll deal with the trays, I'll go get started with the Casto crew over there."

"Hang on a second. Wait for me," Jake said. He took care of our trays, and we walked over to the group together.

"Hey, folks. We were sorry to hear about Bob," I said when we approached the group. There were a few cousins and a handful of friends, most of whom I'd known for years.

"Yeah, it's a real mess," Wes Granger said. It appeared that he was going to be acting as the spokesman for the group.

"Would you all care for some donuts?" I asked as I offered the last box.

"Thanks, but we're stuffed. Who knew a hospital could serve chow this good?"

Calling what Barton prepared "chow" was an insult to the very concept of fine dining, but I wasn't about to correct him.

"That's okay. Take them for later. They make a good snack," I said, offering him the box as Jake and I took seats beside him without being invited.

No one seemed to protest, and one woman even flipped the box open and started pawing through my treats. I decided to ignore her as well. "What exactly happened to Bob?"

"He dislocated his shoulder, cracked a few ribs, and he's got a nasty bump on his head," Wes explained.

"That's terrible," I said. He'd missed the point of my question entirely, so I decided to ask it a different way. "Did he blow out a tire or something?"

"The chief thinks he nodded off behind the wheel, but Bob wouldn't have done that. He was too careful a driver," Wes said, and a few other folks nodded in agreement. "We believe he dodged a deer in the road. It happens more often than you might think."

It was probably the best-case scenario they could come up with to justify the accident, and for all I knew, it could have even been true. Deer loved to come out and graze, especially at night, and it wasn't anything to see them dead on the side of the road where they'd lost the battle with four wheels and steel.

"It happens," Jake said agreeably. "Did you hear that his former business partner is in here, too?"

There was a sudden icy pall over the table, but I didn't blame Jake for asking the question. With this crew, a direct inquiry was the only way we were going to get any answers at all.

"We heard that somebody clobbered him. It was past due, if you ask me," Wes said with a shrug.

"Wesley!" an older woman chided him.

"Well, it's true, Aunt Irma. That man screwed Bob over but good, and we all know it. Who knows how many other people he put the shaft to?" Wes asked.

"He and Bob were fighting recently, weren't they?" Jake

asked. I was trying to keep my voice neutral, but Jake's had slipped into "cop" mode from habit alone. It almost sounded as though Jake was accusing the man of something merely by his tone of voice.

"Maybe so, but he'd have to get in line to take a crack at Van Rayburn," Wes said. "Bob didn't do it, that's for sure."

"How can you be so positive?" I asked gently.

"Because I know Bob Casto," Wes said gruffly. He stood, and the others joined him. I noticed that they left my donut box on the table as they gathered their trays together.

"Don't forget your treats," I said as a gentle reminder.

"Thanks, but like I said, we're fine without them. Come on, folks. Let's go."

Once they were gone, Jake frowned at me. "That was all my fault, wasn't it?"

"Your voice may have been a little too authoritative there at the end," I admitted.

"I'm working on it, but sometimes I can't help but slip into old patterns. It's completely different questioning people when they aren't compelled to answer you. I'm not sure I'm ever going to be able to break those old habits."

I kissed his cheek. "Don't be so hard on yourself. I think you're doing just fine."

Jake merely shrugged as he reached for the donuts. "What should we do with these?"

"Just throw them away," I said, no longer wanting them after they'd been so soundly rejected by the group.

"Are you sure? We still might be able to use them."

"I'm positive," I said as Barton walked out of the kitchen and joined us.

"Hey, you can't bring food into a cafeteria," he said, teasing me.

"You're right," I said as I took the box and chucked it into the nearest can.

Barton looked devastated by my action. "I was just teasing, Suzanne. I'm sorry."

"I didn't throw them out because of you," I told him with a smile. "They served their purpose, at least as much as they could, anyway."

"You're trying to figure out what happened to Van Rayburn, aren't you?" Barton asked softly.

"What makes you say that?" Jake asked him.

"Come on, I won't tell anyone. You asked Emma and her mom to sub for you this morning, and I know for a fact that you're not sick. What else could it be?"

"Maybe I just wanted to spend the day with my husband," I said.

"It looks to me as though you're managing to do both," Barton said, "but that's none of my business."

"Have you heard anything about Van?" I asked him. After all, working where he did, Barton was bound to pick up tidbits every now and then that might be helpful to us in our investigation.

"Well, I know that he's on a pretty bland diet, but at least he's awake," Barton said.

"How about Bob Casto?"

"I couldn't say, since there are no food orders for him at all," Barton said. "Would you like me to give you a call if there's a change in either diet?"

"Sure, if it won't get you in trouble with your bosses here," I said.

"I've got pretty free rein around here these days," the chef said with a grin. "They are all afraid that I'll leave, so I can get away with just about anything, as long as I keep cooking."

"Emma told me that you were planning a pop-up restaurant," I said. "How's that coming?"

"What can I say? It's a work in progress. How was your food today? I spotted you two eating earlier, but I didn't have the chance to come over and chat."

"It was amazing, as always," I said. "I don't know how you do it."

"It's really not all that hard," Barton replied, blushing a little. "It's just simple ingredients prepared with care."

"You don't give yourself enough credit," Jake said. "By the way, you still owe me a catered lunch, you know."

"Give me a day's notice, and I'll be ready whenever you are," Barton said with a grin.

"Chef, we have a problem in the kitchen," one of his underlings said as he approached us.

"What did I tell you before, Gavin?" Barton asked in a serious voice.

"Sorry. There's a situation that needs your attention," he corrected himself.

"Thank you. I'll be there in a minute."

"It's a pretty *important and urgent* situation, Chef," Gavin said, looking a little bit worried about his boss's lack of prompt response.

"I'd better go see what's going on," Barton said to us. "I'll talk to you later."

"Looking forward to it," I said.

After he was gone, I asked Jake, "What do you say? Should we take another shot at Wes and the rest of Bob's family and friends?"

"We could, but I'm not all that sure that it would do any good," Jake said. "Besides, I have something else in mind. What say we go visit the mayor at city hall?"

"Do you think there's anything more we can get out of George?" I asked my husband.

"Not particularly, but while we're there on a legitimate errand, I thought we might drop by Van's office and see if we could find anything that might help us in our investigation."

I kissed Jake, and then I smiled at him. "That's absolutely brilliant. I knew there was a reason I married you."

"Do you mean *besides* my charm and good looks?" he asked, clearly happy about the praise I'd just given him.

"Of course. That all goes without saying," I said as we made our way back to the Jeep.

"Trust me. Feel free to say it anytime you'd like," Jake answered.

CHAPTER 8

"The door's locked," I whispered to Jake as we tried to get into Van's office. "What should we do?"

"We need to figure out a way to get inside. Let me take a look at it," Jake answered. "You keep a lookout for me."

"Should I whistle or something if I see someone coming?" I asked him as I glanced up and down the hallway.

"You can if you want to, but just saying, 'Jake, somebody's coming' is good enough for me," he answered with a grin.

"Okay, Smarty Pants," I said as I stood with my back to him. I could see George's office from where we were standing, but his secretary's desk was empty. Sue Boggs was his latest assistant, and I wondered where she'd wandered off to. It was a good thing for us that she was gone, though.

Beside Van's office on one side was the one reserved for Buford. I was fairly certain that he was still at the hospital, so I tried his door, just in case.

This one happened to be unlocked. "Jake," I whispered.

His head shot up as though he were a gopher coming out of his hole. "Is somebody coming?"

"No, but Buford's door is unlocked."

"That's nice, but we need to get into Van's office, not Buford's," Jake reminded me, as though I needed him to tell me that.

"Is there a chance we can get into it through here?" I asked him as I gestured to the door.

"I don't know, but I suppose it's worth a shot," Jake said as he stood. "This lock is a lot sturdier than I was expecting. What is Van hiding in there?"

"I don't know, but we need to find out," I said.

"Hang on a second," Jake said, and then he examined the lock on Buford's door.

"It's open, remember?" I asked.

"I know, but this lock is older, and it looks more in line with the others in the hallway." He gestured back to Van's. "On the other hand, this one is nearly brand new. Do you see what I mean?"

"I do. Listen, we can stand out here for hours discussing it until someone comes along, but why don't we duck in and see if we can get through to Van's office in the meantime?"

"Sure. Of course. Sorry," he said. "I just found it interesting, that's all."

I suddenly felt bad about chiding him. "It makes me wonder about what he might be hiding, too," I said as I opened Buford's door and stepped inside. Jake was close on my heels, and he shut the door behind us so at least no one would know that we were there.

The room was small, but Buford made up for it by being as neat as he could possibly be. The place was immaculate, and it was difficult for me to believe that anyone could get any work done in such a sterile environment.

Unfortunately, there were no doors there leading to Van's office.

"It's a dead end," I said. "Sorry."

"That's okay," Jake said as we backed out into the hallway.

The only problem was that someone must have spotted us going into Buford's workspace after all.

We'd been caught red-handed, and there was nothing we could do about it.

"What happened? Did you two come looking for me and get lost along the way?" George asked with a wicked grin on his face.

"As a matter of fact, we were just on our way to see you," I said as lightly as I could muster.

"Through Buford's cubbyhole? What did the poor old guy do to merit your attention?"

"The truth is that we were looking for a way into Van's office," I admitted, deciding a little belatedly that honesty might just be the best policy, at least in this case.

"You know, you could have just asked me. I have a key to every door in the building," George replied as he jangled his oversized key ring. After glancing at Van's lock, he frowned. "Huh. That's odd."

"It's new, isn't it?" Jake asked him.

"Yes, and besides that, it's against the rules to change these door locks without written permission from my office. Hang on a second," he said as he grabbed his phone from his pocket. "Denise, I need you up at my office. Sure, that would be fine. Okay." After George hung up, he told us, "Denise Osmond is our new custodial lady. She was born into a family of farmers, and there's nothing around here that she can't fix. This should be a snap for her."

"Since when did Denise start working for the town of April Springs?" I asked.

"Do you know her?" the mayor asked me.

"She's been coming into Donut Hearts for years. At least she did up until six months ago. For some reason, she just stopped showing up. I figured I must have offended her somehow, but I never got the chance to apologize, just in case it was something I said."

"Then you haven't seen her lately?" George asked with a smile.

"Didn't I just say that?" I asked Jake, confused about the mayor's comment.

The moment I saw Denise, all my confusion was ended. The woman must have dropped thirty pounds since I'd seen her last. When she came up the stairs, she was practically trotting. The moment we made eye contact, she said, "Suzanne Hart! Aren't you a sight for sore eyes."

"What happened to you?" I asked her as we hugged. "You look fantastic."

Denise beamed. "You'd think I'd get tired of hearing that, but not so far," she said. "What's up, Mr. Mayor?"

"This lock doesn't meet our specs. Did you have anything to do with installing it?"

She looked at the lock in question and shook her head. "No, sir, I've never seen it before. To be fair, I might not have noticed it, but I surely didn't install it."

"That's all I care about, then. Can you open it?"

"You bet I can," she said without even glancing at it again.

"Don't you even need to study it a little first before you make that claim?" Jake asked her.

"I could, but I wouldn't need to. All I need is my drill and three uninterrupted minutes to take care of it."

"We can arrange that, can't we?" George asked us.

"You bet," I said as Jake nodded in agreement.

It took Denise only two of the three minutes she'd asked for. Using her drill with practiced skill, she had the door lock at her mercy in no time at all. After pulling the entire lockset apart, Denise manipulated something inside the opening, and the door swung inward. "Is there anything else?" she asked with a grin.

"Do we have any extra door handles with locks in storage?" George asked her.

"I'm sure I could rustle something up," she said. "It might take me half an hour to make it happen, though."

"That's perfect. Don't forget to let me have a copy of the key when you're finished," the mayor said.

"Will do," Denise said, and then she smiled at me again. "See you around, Suzanne."

"I hope so," I said.

"If I know her, it will take her under ten minutes before she comes back. Can you do much with that time?" George asked us quietly.

"We'll take whatever we can get," Jake said.

"Then start your clocks right now," George said. "Come see me when you're finished."

"You're not coming in with us?" I asked him, in all honesty a little bit relieved.

"It might not be prudent if someone were to catch me snooping around my main rival's office while he's laid up in the hospital," George said.

"Good thinking. That's why you're the mayor instead of one of us," I said.

"Tick tock, tick tock," George reminded us.

It was all the push we needed.

Nobody was going to be outside standing guard this time.

Jake and I were going to search the office together.

While Buford's workspace was immaculate, Van's was a real mess. Papers were strewn everywhere, and files were stacked up in every available nook and cranny. "How are we going to do this in just ten minutes?" I asked Jake.

"Hurriedly, and yet still with as much care as possible. We don't have time to consult each other with what we find. Take photos with your phone, and I'll do the same. We can share our notes after we're finished."

"That sounds like a plan to me," I said. I started scanning the desktop as I pulled out my phone. On the very top of the pile was a form that looked extremely official. None of it had been filled out yet, but the heading was enough to get my attention, and it took everything I had not to shout to Jake what I'd found. I took a few pictures of it, and then I continued to dig as Jake went through the stacks on the chairs. Digging down into the mess, there was a great deal of official correspondence, but none of it looked pertinent to our case. Still, I took a few more photos until I found a credit card bill at the very bottom. Opening it up, I couldn't help but whistle out loud when I saw its outstanding balance, as well as the bold PAST DUE stamped in, appropriately enough, red ink. The minimum payment alone would have drained our joint bank account.

"What did you find?" Before I could reply, Jake added, "Strike that. Back to work."

I nodded as I took a few shots of the bill. At least it was itemized. There might be a few clues hidden in it, but that would have to wait until later.

I noticed that Jake must have found a few things himself, because he was busy taking a few photos along the way himself.

I opened the top drawer in the middle of the desk and found a greeting card. How nice. Then I read it, and I immediately changed my mind. The front of the card, which I photographed, featured a flowery heart with the words "*I Missed You*" embossed on it. Inside was written, "*But My Aim is Improving, So Watch Out.*" Below it, in a woman's handwriting, it read, "Don't push me away, Van. You won't like what happens if you try." It was signed simply, "Vivian."

Wow. My hands shook a little as I photographed the evidence before putting it back where I found it. I was about to say something to Jake when I heard footsteps approaching from the hallway. "Denise is coming back!"

"I'm nearly finished," Jake said, and we both barely managed to make it out into the hallway before she arrived.

"I'm surprised to find you two still here," she said with a

frown as she approached us. There was an old, dull lockset in one hand and a toolbox in the other.

"We didn't want to leave Van's office unguarded," I said. It was the first thing that sprang into my mind. I just hoped she bought it.

"That's very considerate of you both," Denise said with a smile, "but I've got it from here. Nobody is going to get into this office without a key from now on."

"Unless they have a cordless drill of their own," Jake joked.

Denise must not have found it very funny. "If they damage this lockset, they'll have to answer to me."

Jake started toward George's office, but I lingered for a moment. "May I ask you something, Denise?"

"Go ahead and shoot, as long as you don't mind me working while we chat. I've got a list a mile long to do today, and this isn't helping matters any."

"What do you think of Van Rayburn?" I asked.

Denise frowned for a moment before answering. "It's not my policy to answer questions like that, Suzanne," she said, clearly scolding me.

"I'm sorry," I said, sorry that I'd pushed her. "I was just curious."

"No worries." She frowned at the door for a moment before she added, "But since we go way back, I will say that I wouldn't trust him any farther than I could throw him. The truth is that I'm not a big fan of politicians in general."

"You certainly chose an odd place to work," I said.

"Does that opinion include the mayor?" Jake asked her.

She smiled at the first mention of George. "Him I like. He used to be a cop, you know."

"We do," Jake said. "As a matter of fact, so did I."

"I know that, too," she said as she winked at Jake. "Now,

if you two will excuse me, this doorknob isn't going to install itself."

As she got to work, Jake and I moved away from her, but we weren't ready to tackle the mayor just yet.

We needed to find somewhere we could compare notes on what we'd found first. I tugged on Jake's arm and said, "Care for a quick stroll downstairs?"

"George is waiting for us, remember?" my husband reminded me.

"He can wait a little longer," I insisted. "We need to share what we found in there with each other before we tell anyone else."

"Did you find something related to him?" Jake asked.

"Downstairs," I insisted.

"Okay," Jake agreed. We headed for the stairs, and once we were on the ground level, I found an unoccupied bench in the hallway.

"Over there looks good," I said, and we claimed our seats.

"Do you want to go first, or should I?" Jake asked.

I knew that I wouldn't be able to wait for my turn. "Let me," I said as I pulled out my phone and started scrolling through the photos I'd just taken in Van's office.

"Look at this," I told Jake as I thrust my phone toward him.

"It's a formal letter of impeachment," Jake said in wonder. "Van was trying to get rid of George, wasn't he?"

"That's what it looks like to me. It's still blank, though. Maybe he changed his mind about going after the mayor."

"Based on everything I've heard about Van, I'm guessing that he just hasn't had time to fill it out yet. This doesn't look good for George."

"We have to tell him about it," I said. "And Chief Grant needs to know, too."

"All in good time," Jake said. "What else did you find?"

"A credit card bill that backs up what we've heard about the man. It appears that Van really is stone cold broke, if this is any indication. I'd like to take some time to go through his charges, but suffice it to say that the overall picture is pretty bleak."

Jake shook his head when he saw the charged amount. "I'm having trouble believing that anyone can run up a bill that high in just one month. That's good detective work, Suzanne. Did you find anything else of interest?"

"I also stumbled upon the creepiest greeting card I've ever seen in my life," I said. As I pulled up the photos of Vivian's card, I said, "It's certainly not what I was expecting."

"Funny, but it doesn't surprise me at all," Jake said after reading the sentiment expressed inside. "Anything else?"

"No, that's it," I admitted. "Now, let's see what you came up with."

Jake pulled out his own phone as I put mine away. "I found two things that could be important," he said as he showed me the photos. The first one was of a handwritten letter Van had composed but not sent yet, though it had a stamp and an address on the outer envelope. It was addressed to his sister, and the next photo showed the letter itself. *"Noreen, I've told you before, but it bears repeating. I am through bailing you out. If you're going to keep getting yourself in these financial messes, you've got to take responsibility for your own actions. It's like I told you today when we had lunch, you're not getting another dime from me, so you might as well stop asking."*

"Wow, she must have really been pushing him for money," I said.

"And what's more, he keeps turning her down. Motive for murder, perhaps?"

"You know it. He might have been refusing her because he's broke himself, but it appears that he hasn't told Noreen that yet."

"What else did you find?" I asked him.

Jake frowned for an instant before he spoke. "You're not going to like this one."

"I can handle whatever it is," I told him.

Jake nodded as he pulled up the last photo on his phone. It was an invitation to dinner from Gabby, written in her distinctive hand, promising a meal beyond his dreams. That wasn't the bad part, though.

Van had scrawled across the face of the note, "Dump her ASAP!"

"There you are," George said as he suddenly loomed in front of us. "Did you forget about me?"

"We were just on our way up," I said.

"Save your lies for your real suspects, Suzanne," George said with a grin. "Let's take a walk, shall we? This place has too many folks eager to see me fall."

CHAPTER 9

"**S**o, what did you find?" George asked us as we all sat out on the bench by the town clock. That particular spot had some bad memories for me, but then again, there was barely a place left in April Springs that didn't call up something that I would rather forget. To be fair though, there were also so many happy memories in town that I tried to dwell on instead. Not three hundred yards from the spot where we now sat, I'd taken my first bike ride, had my first kiss, and earned my first real money as a grown-up.

"You're not going to like it," Jake said, pulling me from my thoughts.

"Why would I expect otherwise? Did the man have a voodoo doll of me in his desk drawer?"

"No," I said, "but we did find a form for a formal impeachment."

George stood suddenly and started pacing near us. "That idiot was actually going through with it? I thought he'd gotten over that weeks ago."

"What was there for him to get over?" Jake asked softly.

"Van accused me of taking bribes in exchange for my influence. Tell me, what influence do I have worth paying for? I told him he was way off base, and I thought he'd forgotten all about it."

"Evidently not," I said. "That form was on top of his desk,

so it appears it was on the top of his to-do list. That doesn't look good for you."

"Don't you think I know that, Suzanne?" George protested loudly.

"Take it easy, Mr. Mayor," Jake said evenly. "We're all on the same side here, remember?" My husband had a way of speaking softer than normal and getting more attention than if he'd been shouting. It was something I would have loved to learn how to do myself.

"Sorry," George told me, and I nodded in acceptance. "It's just so frustrating. I wish Van could remember who attacked him and get me off the hook. You wouldn't believe the calls I've been fielding already."

"I'm guessing they aren't offering you their support," I said.

"A few of them are, but most of them are implying that I'm not fit to be mayor if I go around attacking everyone who disagrees with me. It's like they don't even know me."

"I know it's difficult, but you really have to keep your cool, now more than ever," I said.

"I get it. It's just easier said than done."

"You need to find a way to make it happen, though," Jake admonished him.

"So, what else did you uncover?" George asked. "Was there anything else about me? I'm surprised Van didn't have a frame-up all ready for me."

"We didn't find anything in his office, but we haven't searched his cottage yet," Jake said.

George's frown grew even deeper. "Do you think there's something there, too?"

"Who knows?" Jake asked. "We won't know until we get in, though I'm not exactly sure how we're going to accomplish that."

"You'll think of something. I'm sure of it," George said. "So, what did you uncover about my fellow suspects? You've got to at least give me something to make my day go a little better."

I was about to say something when someone called out to us from across the street.

Chief Grant was striding purposefully toward us, and it didn't appear that he just wanted to pass the time of day.

"Mr. Mayor, do you have a second?" the chief asked as he neared us.

"We're kind of in the middle of something," George said. "Can it wait?"

"It's okay. Go talk to him," I said, taking the opportunity to get away. I wasn't all that thrilled about sharing our new information with the mayor, and the police chief had just given Jake and me a perfect excuse. "We'll catch up with you later."

"Actually, I'd appreciate it if you'd stick around as well," Chief Grant said. "Why don't you wait for me across the street?"

"Anything you need to say to me, you can say in front of them," George said firmly.

"Are you sure about that?"

"Positive," the mayor said.

"Fine. Have it your way. Van is starting to remember the attack," Chief Grant said.

"Don't tell me. He thinks I did it, doesn't he?"

"It's nothing that concrete. Early this morning he was eating a bowl of ice cream when someone came to his door. He remembers opening it to see who it was, but that's when everything fades to black."

"Why are you telling me this?" George asked. "I wasn't there, and I certainly didn't do it, so I can't help you."

"I just thought you'd want to know," the chief said. Was that really true, though? He'd been watching the mayor carefully as he'd told him that Van's memory was coming back. Was he hoping to see some kind of slip in the mayor's demeanor? I was beginning to believe that the police chief was actually entertaining the possibility that George had actually attacked his political rival!

"Well, you told me, so now I know," George said. "Now, if you'll excuse us, we were just discussing something else."

"Is it related to the attack on Van?" the chief asked.

I could see George start to deny it, something that I was determined not to let happen. "Yes," I blurted out before the mayor could contradict me.

George didn't look particularly happy about my interjection, but there was nothing he could do about it at that point.

"Is there something you need to share with me, Suzanne?" the chief asked.

I made an executive decision on the spot, without consulting George or Jake. "Yes. We were looking around Van's office, and we found several things that you are going to want to know about."

Jake frowned for just a moment, but as quickly as that, he was on board. "It should help broaden the scope of your investigation."

"If you don't mind, I'll be the judge of that," the chief said, openly scowling. "That was the second reason I was hunting the mayor down. Denise told me that he had a key to Van's office. I didn't realize you two already beat me to it."

"We didn't take anything, if that counts," Jake said.

"Nothing but photographs," I amended.

It was Jake's turn to glance at me askance. Apparently I wasn't making either man very happy with me.

"You know what? I'm not going to do this on the street corner. Come with me."

"Are you talking to me or them?" George asked.

"To all of you. Come on. Let's go."

We really had no choice but to follow the chief of police across the street and back inside city hall.

Once we were in front of Van's office, the police chief turned to the mayor and held out his hand. "The key, please."

George found the proper key, and after the door lock was taken care of, Chief Grant held out his hand. "I'll take that, if you don't mind."

"I need these keys," the mayor protested.

"You don't need Van's. As far as I'm concerned, you can keep the rest. Just give me his key."

George clearly didn't like it, but he didn't really have any choice, either. Taking the key off his ring, he handed it over grumpily. "Let's go see what this is all about."

The chief didn't budge, though. "I'm sorry, but you can't come in."

That was the last straw as far as George was concerned. "Need I remind you, Chief Grant, that you serve at my pleasure? I can fire you without notice if I'm so inclined."

"Sure, you can get rid of me, and a part of me wishes that you'd do just that, but you can't tell me what to do. I'll run this investigation, and my entire department, as I see fit unless and until I am relieved of my duties. Do I make myself clear?"

I glanced over at Jake and saw him trying to hide a smile. I was positive my husband would have reacted the exact same way if he'd been in Chief Grant's position.

George scowled for a moment at being balked, and then he said in a huff, "Never mind. I've got things to do myself, important things."

He turned and headed to his office without another word to any of us.

Jake nodded in the chief's direction. "Nicely handled."

"You taught me yourself that I can't afford to let anyone push me around while I'm on the job." Jake started to smile until the chief added, "That includes you, too."

"I wasn't pushing you around," Jake protested.

"Maybe not, but you were pushing your luck instigating that lock change and then snooping around while you waited for Denise to get the new hardware."

Jake shrugged. "We didn't see any harm in it."

"I suppose not, but I should have seen the place first," the chief admitted. "The problem is that I'm being pulled in so many different directions at the moment that I can't do everything!"

"That's why you need to delegate," Jake said softly.

"I have good people on my staff, but there's not a single one of them that I would trust with this investigation."

"Sometimes you have to let go, though," Jake added.

"Maybe. If so, I haven't acquired the knack yet."

"Do you need us for this?" I asked the chief. "If you don't, we have some things we should be doing ourselves."

"Sorry, but that's going to have to wait. You two are coming inside with me. I want to see what you found, firsthand."

It was most likely a little unorthodox, but he was the chief of police, so what choice did we really have?

"I'm not going to repeat the steps you took. I don't have time for it. What exactly did you find significant?" he asked as he stared at the messy office. "Suzanne, you go first."

I picked up the impeachment form and handed it to him. "I suppose this is first on my list."

The chief took it, studied it for a second, and then handed it back to me. "It's blank."

"Apparently Van has been threatening to impeach the mayor for some time."

That caught Chief Grant by surprise. "On what grounds?"

"Selling his influence," Jake said.

That got a momentary grin from the police chief. "I can't imagine it being worth much."

"Not to play devil's advocate, or try to hang my friend, but you'd be surprised," I said. I didn't particularly want to share my views with the police chief, but he needed to know how serious the charge could be. "The last mayor was murdered over doing something exactly like that," I said. "You'd be shocked by how much sway the mayor has. He can influence a great many things, some of them worth hundreds of thousands of dollars to the right people. You need to take the charge seriously."

"So I gather," the chief said as he nodded. Jake looked at me and nodded as well, offering his approval of my disclosure. After all, it wouldn't do to be caught holding back the form's significance later. "What else did you find?"

I pulled out the threatening greeting card from Vivian and handed it to him. He took it, flipped it open, and frowned as he read the message inside. "She sounds like a real prize, doesn't she?"

"If I got a card like that, I know that I'd certainly be watching my back," I said.

"What else?"

"We found Van's credit card bill," I said as I retrieved that as well.

The chief seemed reluctant to take it. "That's his private property."

"I know that, but it proved one rumor we've heard that the man is on the verge of bankruptcy."

"It's as bad as all that?" the chief asked.

"You can either take my word for it or see for yourself," I said.

The chief nodded, opened the statement, and quickly took in the gist of it. "That doesn't help explain why someone attacked Van."

"Unless he owed money to more than a credit card company," Jake said suddenly.

We hadn't even discussed that possibility up until that moment, but I could see why Jake might suspect it. Why hadn't that thought even occurred to me? It was certainly something else we needed to consider.

"Maybe," the chief said. "What have you got, Jake?"

It was time for my husband to take over. "I found a letter going out to Noreen about a loan refusal, which matches what we've heard about their relationship as well. She's next to broke herself, and apparently she was expecting Van to bail her out yet again. He refused her time and time again, and we believe she doesn't realize that her brother is broke as well."

"That would be solid grounds for murder, or attempted murder, at any rate, if she's set to inherit his estate, whatever it might amount to," the chief said. "You both did good work."

I saw Jake hesitate, not wanting to add the incriminating evidence about Gabby Williams, but I couldn't let him do that. Perhaps he was simply waiting for me to chime in.

"There's one more thing," I said. "Show him, Jake."

My husband nodded as he handed the chief Gabby's dinner invitation, along with the scrawled note that Van was going to dump her. "Wow. It's a wonder to me it took this long for someone to take a run at Van Rayburn," the chief said. "Is that everything, or is anyone else after the head councilman?"

"Not that we know of," I said.

"I'll have someone go through the rest of this, but I appreciate your insights," the chief said.

"Since we're sharing information," Jake said slyly, "were you able to find anything at Van's cottage that might help the investigation?"

"Yours or mine?" the chief asked guardedly.

"Why can't it be both?" Jake asked him.

"I don't know why it matters. I didn't find anything incriminating about anyone when I checked the place out earlier. It's a dead end, at least as far as I'm concerned."

"Do you really think Van will ultimately remember who attacked him?" I asked the chief.

"You'd have to ask his doctors," Chief Grant said. "I'll leave the diagnoses up to them." As he looked around the messy office, he asked, "I assume you both have a game plan of attack from here on out. Am I right?"

"We haven't really discussed anything that detailed yet," Jake said levelly. I suppose on one level it was true, but it didn't actually take a conference to decide what came next. We needed to take another run at our suspects now that we were armed with new information that had been confirmed by outside sources. It might end up being a huge waste of time if Van recovered his memories, but if he didn't, the sooner the culprit was nailed down, the better. Until that happened, it was not that hard to imagine that the councilman was in more danger than ever. "We've been forthright with you. Can you at least give us something that might help us?"

Chief Grant appeared to think about it for a few moments before he finally said, "We've got the time of the attack down to a four-hour window. Van spoke with Harry Milner around eleven about an item on the council agenda, and you found him a little after three. I don't know if that helps, but it's something. Who are you going after next?"

"We honestly haven't decided," I said.

"But you've got an idea, surely," the chief said. "You know

what? Never mind. If I don't know what you're up to, I can't forbid you from doing it. Keep in touch though, okay?"

"You bet," Jake said.

As the police chief walked down the hall toward the mayor's office, I turned to my husband. "I'm guessing you have more of an idea of what comes next than you let on just now."

"How well you know me," Jake said with a soft grin. "Are you ready to roll?"

"I'm right behind you," I replied with a smile of my own.

CHAPTER 10

O NCE WE WERE BACK OUT in my Jeep, I asked Jake, "Where should we start? Should we keep looking for new clues or speak with our suspects again?"

"I vote for heading to the hospital," Jake said. "After all, unless I miss my guess, that's where most of our suspects are right now."

"Sounds good to me," I said as I started the engine and began driving. "Do you really think a loan shark might have attacked Van?"

"No, not really," Jake said. "The more I think about it, it just doesn't make sense."

"Why not?"

"If the shark wanted Van to pay on his loan, what sense would it make hitting him in the back of the head and possibly killing him? That's no way to get your money back. If Van had a broken leg, some cracked ribs, or a busted arm, it might be more plausible. Heck, even if he'd been beaten up, it might tell us that was what happened, but besides his head wound, there wasn't an obvious bruise on him."

"Does it ever bother you knowing all of that?" I asked him.

"Suzanne, I know a great many things that are much worse than how a loan shark works."

"I get that. I just don't think I could do it."

"Well," he said with a slight smile, "if it's any consolation,

I couldn't make a donut to save my life. We each have our own talents."

I wanted to press him more on how he coped with all of the darkness he'd seen in his professional life, but at that moment, his phone rang.

"It's Ellie," he told me. "I've got to take this."

"Be my guest," I said, trying not to show any emotion. Ellie had a habit of acquiring married men, but I was going to make sure that she didn't add my husband to her collection. However, I knew that if I said anything overtly, Jake would just think that I didn't trust him. Him I trusted just fine. It was that man-eater I had a problem with.

After a brief conversation, Jake hung up and turned to me. He was clearly waiting for me to ask about his little chat, but I wasn't about to do that.

"Who should we tackle first? Should we set someone in our sights, or take whoever comes our way first?" I asked him.

"You're not even going to ask me about that call?" Jake asked me.

"It's none of my business. After all, she won you, fair and square."

"Suzanne, nobody *won* anyone. We're having lunch tomorrow, if that's okay with you."

"I don't have a problem with it," I said, "but Barton might."

"It's his afternoon off. She's already touched base with him." Jake was looking at me curiously the entire time we spoke.

"Good. Then that's settled."

Jake's frown deepened. "Seriously? You aren't going to say a word?"

I had to laugh. His reaction to my lack of one had turned out better than anything I could have said to him. "Jake, I trust you," I said, not adding the second half of that thought about Ellie's reliability.

"I appreciate that, but even you have to admit that she's a pretty woman," he said.

I pulled the Jeep over, much to his surprise. "Do you *want* me to complain? Barton's going to be there, too, right?"

"He's kind of essential, since he's doing the cooking," Jake admitted.

"Then you've got a chaperone built right in. But do me a favor, would you?"

"Anything," Jake said.

"If she makes the slightest pass at you during your lunch, tell her to start looking over her shoulder, because I'll be gunning for her."

Jake laughed. "Now that's what I was looking for."

I stuck my tongue out at him, and then I laughed as well. I truly wasn't worried about Ellie. My husband loved me, and I knew it.

We were at the hospital soon enough, and I pulled into an empty space in the visitors' lot. "Let's go try to find Van's attacker," I said as I locked up the Jeep.

"I hope we can," Jake said worriedly. "I honestly don't like not knowing who did it."

"Why is that?"

"I can't help wondering why they haven't tried again. After all, the attacker has more incentive than ever to make another run at Van. After all, if the councilman gets his memory back, whoever went after the man is sunk."

"The chief said he'd put a guard on his room," I reminded Jake.

"I hope he follows through, but with as many ways as he's being pulled right now, it could have easily slipped his mind."

I patted my husband's shoulder. "We'll make sure that it doesn't, okay?"

"Okay," he said. "Suzanne, I'm really happy that you're in my life."

"I feel the same way about you," I said happily. I hadn't realized it, but before Jake had come along, I'd led an ordinary existence, with highs and lows of its own, but until we'd found each other, I hadn't realized just how much I'd been missing out on before, even when I'd been married to Max.

"You aren't going to get in to see him unless you crawl over my dead body!" Noreen shouted at Vivian as we walked down the hall toward Van's room. Were those two women honestly *still* fighting? At least Gabby wasn't there joining in the fray. To my relief, a police officer was stationed outside Van's room, but he made no attempt to intervene in the argument. As a matter of fact, he looked as though he might be enjoying the distraction.

"Don't tempt me," Vivian shouted back. "He wants to see me!"

"In your dreams!" Noreen answered.

"Ladies, please," Buford said, still trying to play the role of peacemaker, though obviously he was out of his depth with these two fireballs. "Let's show some decorum."

"You can take your decorum and shove it where the sun doesn't shine, errand boy," Vivian said, turning angrily on him.

"Oh, that's a nice mouth you've got yourself there," Noreen answered smugly.

"I wasn't talking to you, hag," Vivian said. "You're a leech and a parasite, and Van doesn't need you in his life. Go find another money tree, loser."

Noreen's face turned white at the insult. It must have really hit home. She snapped back, "You're just rubbish. He threw you away, but you don't have the common sense to take the hint. Why don't you do us all a favor and go sink your fangs into someone else?"

Vivian took that to heart, and she reared back to slap

Noreen. The only problem was that Buford got in the way at precisely the wrong moment, and Vivian's hand connected with his cheek instead. The sound of the contact was enough to catch everyone's attention within ten yards, and an angry white patch lit up Buford's face as though it had been painted with a brush.

"Now see what you've done," Noreen said, turning to Buford. "You've managed to attack Van's best friend, too."

"He's not his best friend, but I didn't mean to hit him," Vivian said. "I was aiming for you."

"What a surprise that you missed me," Noreen said, unconsciously echoing Vivian's greeting card message I'd found earlier.

"Just give me another shot. I promise that I won't miss the next time," she said in a growl that barely sounded like words.

"That's it," a security guard said as he approached. "You three. Out. Right now."

"What did I do?" Buford protested. "I was trying to get them to stop."

"Well, you failed miserably at it, didn't you?" the guard said.

"Sir, do you have any idea who I am? I am a powerful man in this town."

"Tell it to someone who cares, pal. You're a part of this group disturbing the peace, and I have every right to remove you." He turned to the patrol officer and asked, "Right?"

"Don't ask me. I'm just here guarding the door," the officer said.

The security guard took that as agreement. "I'm not wrong. Now let's go. You can come back after you've all cooled down some, but not for at least an hour. Am I making myself clear?"

"Fine," Noreen snapped, "but I'm not leaving until she does."

"You're *all* going," the guard said, and it was clear he'd had enough. All three left the hospital, glaring at each other as they went. Just to be sure, the security guard followed them out, leaving Jake and me standing there with the cop. Jake and I tagged along with the ejected group, hoping to get a word with Buford. Once we were all outside, Jake pulled the councilman aside. "Do you know anything about Van wanting to impeach the mayor?" he asked.

"I thought he was over that," Buford said, frowning. "Surely he's not trying to bring that up again. The man clearly has it in for our mayor, and the feeling is mutual."

"That leaves you in the middle again, doesn't it?" I asked him.

"No, not anywhere close. I know where my loyalties lie," he responded.

Noreen clearly wasn't happy about us chatting. "Buford, are you coming?"

"I'll be right there," he said as he hurried to her.

"That was something to see, wasn't it?" I asked Jake as we walked back inside.

"Tell me about it," he replied.

When we got to the police officer, Jake asked, "How long were they fighting, anyway?"

"Since I got on duty an hour ago," the man answered.

"At least this job isn't boring, right?" I asked.

"It's been a better show than what's usually playing on television these days," he admitted.

Jake said, "You're new, aren't you? I'm Jake Bishop, and this is my wife, Suzanne Hart."

He took Jake's hand and then mine. "I know who you both are. I'm Dan Bradley," he said in reply.

"Nice to meet you, Officer," I said as I started for the door.

He didn't budge, though.

"Would you mind stepping aside? We'd like to speak with Van for a moment," Jake said.

"Sorry, but I've got my orders. No one goes in without the

chief's permission," the officer explained. "Unless you're on the hospital staff, there aren't any exceptions."

"Get your boss on the line and ask him," Jake said, clearly unhappy about being thwarted.

The officer frowned for a moment. "Hang on." After a whispered conversation, Officer Bradley said, "Go on in."

"Thanks," I said, but Jake merely nodded until I jabbed him in the ribs.

He quickly added, "Thank you, Officer Bradley."

"You're welcome, sir," the young man said, relieved that my husband was at least being civil about it.

"Jake, he's just doing his job," I whispered as we walked into the room.

"I know that," Jake answered.

I decided not to push it.

Van was sitting up in bed doing the crossword puzzle. "What's a seven-letter word for investment?"

"'Money' is too short," I said, and then I added, "Try 'capital.'"

Van smiled. "That's it. What brings you two by? Do you know why all of the excitement outside suddenly died? I'm already starting to miss it."

"Your sister and your ex-girlfriend were fighting about you, and Buford had the misfortune of trying to get in between them and force them to behave themselves."

Van shook his head. "There's no way he managed to do that, did he? That man couldn't stop a group of kindergartners from taking a nap."

"All three of them were thrown out of the hospital, at least for the next hour," I said. "I thought you and Buford were friends."

"We are, I suppose," Van said, his frown getting even deeper. "We've had our problems in the past, though. He thinks he should have my job. Did you know that?"

"No, I was under the impression that he was your biggest fan," Jake said.

"Maybe once upon a time, but now that he's gotten a taste of power, he seems to enjoy it a little too much for my taste. That's not going to fly with me once I get out of here," Van said a little cryptically.

"When might that be?" I asked him. "Have the doctors told you anything?"

"Probably, but I must have already forgotten it," Van said, and then he chuckled, clearly pleased with his own attempted cleverness mocking his memory loss.

"You still don't have any idea who attacked you?" Jake asked him.

"I have some thoughts," he admitted. "After all, there's not much else to think about locked up in here. Did you see the guard out front?"

"We did. He's there for your own protection," Jake explained.

"Does the police chief really think that whoever tried to kill me is going to come back for another shot?" Van asked.

"It's a distinct possibility, if you ask me. I endorsed it myself," Jake said.

Van didn't seem pleased that Jake hadn't backed him up. "I think it's a great deal of worry over nothing. My attacker, whoever it might be, wouldn't dream of trying anything here."

"So, you still don't remember who conked you?" I asked him.

"No, and it's driving me crazy. I can remember someone coming to the door, and I know that we had an angry conversation. I must have let them into the house. How else could they get the award to hit me with it? Evidently I was foolish enough to turn my back on whoever it was, and they took advantage of the situation."

"You don't even have a glimmer of who it was?" I asked him.

"Like I said, it's a complete blank."

"Would you care to share your list of suspects with us?" Jake asked.

"Are you two digging into this yourselves?" he asked warily.

I wasn't sure how to answer that, but Jake did it for the both of us. "We just don't want to see whoever did it come back and finish the job."

"Thanks, though I'm surprised you care about me one way or the other." After a momentary pause, Van added, "Strike that. You're worried about the mayor, aren't you? You don't want to see your friend prosecuted for attacking me."

"Especially since he wasn't the one who did it," I said, being a little more adamant than I probably should have been.

"Maybe. Maybe not," Van said.

"About that list," Jake said when a doctor came in. He was scowling about something, and seeing us didn't brighten his mood any.

"You'll both have to leave. I need to examine my patient."

There was no arguing with that. "Okay, but we'll be back," I told Van.

"Until I recover my memory, at least enough to remember who hit me, there's no need for that. In fact, I'm asking you to drop your unofficial investigation right here and now. Let the police handle it."

"You're certainly free to ask us anything you'd like to," Jake said.

"I mean it!" Van said, clearly agitated by my husband's response. "I don't want you digging around in my life."

"Why? Are you afraid of what we might find?" I asked him sweetly.

"Get out!" Van shouted.

"You two need to leave right now," the doctor ordered. "You're clearly upsetting my patient."

"He's not nearly as upset as he's going to be once we figure out what's going on," I said. Was that a glimpse of momentary fear in Van's eyes when I said it?

The door opened, and Officer Bradley stepped in. "Is there a problem here?"

"No. We were just leaving," Jake said.

"For now," I added, more out of spite than anything else.

Once we were out in the hallway, I asked Jake something that had just crossed my mind. "Jake, is it possible that Van *knows* who clobbered him last night?"

Jake looked surprised by my question. "If he knew that, why wouldn't he tell the police?"

"What if he plans on dealing with it himself?" I asked.

"What makes you ask that?"

"I thought I caught a hint of something in his eyes a moment ago," I admitted. "It's nothing I can be sure of, but I think it's at least within the realm of possibility."

"If it's true, then I'm doubly glad there's a guard on his door," Jake said.

"Why is that?"

"It will serve to keep Van inside as well as keeping the bad guy out," Jake said. "What's our next move?"

"Let's go see if Bob Casto is in any better shape to talk than he was earlier," I suggested.

"That sounds like a plan to me," Jake replied, and we went off in search of Van's former business partner's room.

CHAPTER 11

"**H**ANG ON A SECOND," I told Jake as we approached Bob Casto's room. The door had been propped open, and there were several voices coming from inside. We lingered outside in the hallway for a few moments, and sure enough, Casto himself finally spoke.

"I would have gotten away with it, too, if I hadn't had a bit of bad luck in the end."

"Quiet down, Bob!" Wes Granger said urgently. "You're still out of your mind on drugs."

"You quiet down, Wes. I've never seen things clearer in my entire life," Bob answered. "I'm telling you the truth. I'm not one bit sorry about it, either. He deserved exactly what he got."

"Robert!" Aunt Irma said.

"It's true. Every last bit of it!"

We were waiting for Casto to incriminate himself further when Wes popped his head out through the door opening. He got up in Jake's face, and I wondered if the man really was foolish enough to try to intimidate my husband. "How long have you been standing there listening in on a private conversation?"

"How much privacy could you really expect with the door propped wide open?" Jake asked him, never flinching or backing up even one inch. "That was quite an interesting talk you were having just now."

"Bob's out of his mind on drugs," Wes said, stepping back and taking a gentler tone than he had before. "You can't believe anything he's saying. Half an hour ago, he claimed to be a pitcher for the New York Yankees."

"I don't know. He seemed pretty lucid just now to me," I said.

"It kind of sounded as though he were confessing to attacking Van Rayburn."

"He wasn't even talking about Van," Wes said haltingly. There was little doubt the man was lying to protect his cousin.

"It was about something else entirely."

"Sure it was," Jake said, the tone of his voice proving that he didn't believe it for one second. Neither did I.

"Clearly you weren't standing there all that long. A few minutes ago he was telling us all about nearly screwing some guy named Pickering in Union Grove in a land deal that would have netted him twenty grand in three days."

"What was the bad luck at the end?" I asked.

"The guy's secretary, some woman named Hickman, reread the contracts before she'd let him sign the last version, and she found the loophole Bob had slipped in at the last second. Our family and theirs have had a feud for years, but Pickering let his greed get the better of him, and Bob was determined to take advantage of it. That wasn't about Van Rayburn at all."

"Why don't we believe you?" Jake asked him.

"Go to Union Square and ask the man yourself. He'll tell you it's true." Wes stepped back into the room as he added, "Now, if you'll excuse me, it's family and friends only in Bob's room right now."

If he could have slammed the door, I was sure that he would have, but the hospital's doors were designed not to slam even under the most trying circumstances.

"Could he be telling the truth?" I asked Jake once we were alone in the hallway again.

"I suppose anything is possible," he said as he pulled out his phone.

"Who are you calling?"

Jessica Beck

"I've got a friend in the Union Square police department who owes me a favor," he said. "Give me one second."

It didn't surprise me to learn that Jake had cultivated friendships on the various local police forces, especially since he'd once been the interim chief of the April Springs squad. After a few minutes, he rejoined me.

"What did he say?" I asked.

"He knows the parties involved, so he's going over to Pickering's office to get confirmation right now. I suspect that it's true, though. Jan knows the man, and he has a running grudge with half the town."

"Is Jan a man or a woman?" I asked with a smile.

"He's a man. Why, does it matter?"

"No, I was just curious," I said.

Jake raised an eyebrow in my direction. "Suzanne, why are you suddenly so jumpy about me being around other women?"

I thought about what he asked before I automatically denied it. There was a little truth in what he'd just asked me. "I guess I don't like the idea of you having lunch with Ellie," I finally admitted.

"Just because she's a woman? Would you feel the same way if Grace had won me in the auction instead?"

"First of all, as you pointed out earlier, Ellie didn't *win* you. It's important that you remember that. Second, you're free to have lunch with whomever you please. Ellie's a barracuda, though. I wouldn't even trust her with my stepfather."

"I have trouble believing she'd go after Phillip," Jake said with the hint of a grin.

"It's not funny, Jake."

"Not even just a little?" he asked me, a full-blown smile on his face now.

I couldn't resist. I smiled in return. "I know I'm just being silly. Do you forgive me?"

"There's nothing to forgive," he said as he wrapped his arms around me and kissed me soundly. "Woman, there's no one else for me but you, plain and simple. Okay?"

"Okay," I said happily.

"Hey, if you two are going to keep that up, you should get a room," a familiar voice said just down the hallway.

Jake and I broke our embrace as we both turned to see Grace Gauge approaching.

"What are you doing here?" I asked Grace. We hadn't been spending nearly enough time together lately, and I missed her company. That was the only problem with being so in love with my husband. If I didn't make time for the people in my life who were important to me, they might just end up slipping away.

"As a matter of fact, I was looking for you," she said.

"Well, you found me. What's up?"

Grace glanced at Jake, who got the hint immediately. "Would anybody else like some coffee?" It was becoming his standard excuse for making himself scarce.

"I would," I said, thankful that my husband had picked up on the subtle clue. Why shouldn't he, though? After all, he was still a first-class detective.

"Make it three," Grace said gratefully.

"I'll be back in five minutes," Jake said, and then he looked at Grace and asked, "Or should I make it ten?"

"No, five should be fine," she said as she kissed his cheek. "Thank you."

"Hey, it's just coffee," he said with a smile. I was glad that what I'd told Jake earlier had been true. There hadn't been a single jealous vibe when Grace had kissed my husband. For some reason, Ellie just pushed my buttons.

"Now, what's up?" I asked her once Jake was gone on his self-imposed exile.

"It's about Stephen," Grace said.

Stephen Grant, our illustrious young police chief, also happened to be Grace's boyfriend. "What about him?"

"Have you noticed anything different about him lately?" she asked me earnestly.

"Other than the fact that he's working too hard? No, not that I can think of. Why?"

Grace looked a bit exasperated by my response. "Maybe it's just my imagination."

"Grace, what is it?"

She looked as though she were about to cry. "I don't know. He just seems so distant lately. Did Jake ever act like that when he was chief of police?"

"I'm sure it's nothing," I said, hoping that it was true. The two of them were great together, and I would have liked nothing better than for them to make things work.

"But did Jake ever act aloof when he was working as a cop?"

"No," I had to answer honestly, no matter how much it pained me to do so. I didn't like refuting her theory, but I owed Grace the truth. "But different people handle stress in different ways," I quickly amended.

"Well, he's never handled it like this before. Something's going on with him."

"Have you tried coming out and asking him?" I suggested.

"The direct approach, huh? I've thought about it," she admitted.

"What's stopping you?" I asked.

"Maybe I'm afraid of what his answer will be," she said softly.

There was nothing I could say to that, but there was something I could do. I wrapped my arms around my best friend besides my husband and hugged her fiercely. As I did, I could feel the tears escaping from her, and that went on for at least thirty seconds. She finally calmed though, and as Grace pulled away, she dabbed at her cheeks with a tissue in her hand. "Sorry about that."

"Grace, you have nothing to apologize for. Did that help any?"

She looked at me and smiled slightly. "You know what? It did. At least a little."

"So, are you going to talk to him?"

"I'm not sure I've got the courage," she answered.

"Grace Gauge, you are one of the strongest people I've ever known," I told her.

"But still not as strong as your mother, right?" she asked, getting a little of the sunshine back in her smile.

"Well, that's a pretty high bar. Momma is fierce, you know?"

"You don't have to tell me," she answered as Jake tentatively approached.

"Is this a bad time?" he asked gently. "I can take a few more laps around the hospital, but the coffee might get cold if I do."

"Bring it on," Grace said with a grin. "It's fine."

"Are you sure?" he asked, noting her red eyes and the tissue still clutched in her hand.

"I'm positive," she said as she took one of the paper cups from him. "That's delicious. What does Barton do to this to make it so good?"

"I asked him the same thing just now," Jake admitted. "Apparently he puts a touch of chocolate and a whisper of cinnamon in it. It's pretty wonderful, isn't it?"

"It's so good I'm stealing his recipe for the donut shop," I said after taking a sip of my own.

"I'm sure he'd be glad to give it to you freely," Jake said.

"You're probably right, but what fun would that be? Just

think about how much fun Emma and I will have trying to replicate it."

I realized that it was nearly time for dinner. "Are you hungry, Grace?"

"I'm suddenly famished," she said. There was no doubt in my mind the cathartic release of tears had spurred her hunger. "Should we see what Barton's serving in the cafeteria?"

"He's off duty tonight," Jake said, clearly sad about the fact. "I ran into him on his way out. He's got a date with Emma, so his assistant is cooking dinner."

That was sad news indeed. "Anybody up for the Boxcar Grill?" I suggested.

"That sounds wonderful," Grace said. "I'll follow you there. I parked right behind you in the parking lot."

"Then let's go eat," I said.

As we drove back into town, Jake asked, "Do I even want to know what that was all about?"

"Stephen is being a little distant, and Grace is worried about him," I admitted. I was sure that my best friend wouldn't mind me sharing with Jake. In fact, I knew that she would have expected me to. My husband and I were close friends as well as being married to each other, a very convenient arrangement indeed.

"It's a tough job, and he's still young. Being in charge can take its toll. I'm sure it's nothing."

I had a sudden thought. "You wouldn't talk to him, would you?"

Jake looked instantly uncomfortable about the prospect. "About his *relationship*?"

He made it sound as though I'd asked him to take a bribe. "Come on. It's not that hard."

"Maybe not for you, but we're guys, remember?"

"Just feel him out," I said. "For me?"

"I'll try, but I'm not making any promises," Jake said glumly. I had a hunch that he'd rather face down a mad-dog killer than talk to another guy about his feelings, but I knew just as certainly that he'd do it for me.

"Thanks," I said.

I looked in my rearview mirror and waved at Grace, who was following close behind me. She waved back, and we both grinned like a couple of kids.

"You're lucky to have each other in your lives," Jake said after noticing the exchange. "It's rare to keep a friend as long as you have."

"I plan to continue it, too," I said. "When do you think you'll hear back from Jan about Pickering?"

"That's right. I forgot to tell you. He called while I was out taking our coffee for a walk. It all checks out. He asked around, and it pretty much happened the way Wes described it."

"Okay. Thanks for checking," I said.

"Why don't you look satisfied with the answer?" Jake asked me.

"Even if it's a true story, it doesn't necessarily mean that Casto didn't try to kill Van. You know that, don't you?"

"I do. He stays on our list of suspects."

"Are we *ever* going to start narrowing it down?" I asked as we neared the Boxcar's parking lot.

"Don't worry. We'll get to the bottom of this," Jake said, trying his best to assure me.

"Maybe. I just hope it's in time to save Van from another attack."

"So do I," Jake agreed. "I don't need anybody else haunting my nightmares."

"Do you really have bad dreams about things like that?" I

asked, knowing that there were nights when my husband barely slept but never getting a straight answer about the cause.

"More than I care to admit," he said. "You know, that could be all that's wrong with the chief. He's just feeling the weight of responsibility of his job."

"It didn't seem to bother you, though," I said.

"That's not a fair comparison. Not only am I older, but I've had a great deal more experience in law enforcement than he has. He'll come around. She just needs to give him some time."

"But you'll still talk to him, right?" I asked.

"Right," he agreed. After a moment, he put on a brave face. "Let's go eat. I'm suddenly starving."

"Sounds good to me," I said.

CHAPTER 11

"**D**ON'T YOU EVER COOK ANYMORE?" I asked Momma as we joined them at one of the few tables not completely occupied.

"It's my night to cook," Phillip said proudly. "So I gave Dot the choice. We could eat here, or I could make my killer nine-alarm chili."

"I opted for the safety of my digestive tract," Momma said with a smile.

"I thought you liked my chili," Phillip protested.

She patted her husband's hand. "When I have a cold or the slightest bit of congestion, there's nothing I'd rather have in the world," Momma replied.

"It does tend to clean out your nasal passages, doesn't it?" he asked proudly.

"Why aren't *you* cooking, Suzanne?" Momma asked me. "And don't say you've been at the donut shop all day. I came by for a treat, and Emma told me that you were gone."

"Since when did you start eating donuts?" I asked her. Momma got my treats occasionally, but generally there was more reason than to simply satisfy her sweet tooth when she popped in on me at work.

"I get cravings, too," she said, though she couldn't meet my gaze as she said it.

"Momma, were you checking up on me?"

"I wanted to see if you were investigating the attack on Van Rayburn," Momma admitted.

"Jake and I are poking around a little into it," I admitted.

"Jake, you're working with her?" Momma asked, not able to mask being delighted by the news.

"I am," he admitted.

The look of relief on her face wasn't going to go unquestioned. "Momma, I'm perfectly capable of investigating things on my own. Besides, Grace is always there to back me up in case I need help."

"You girls have your own special skill sets, but goodness, your husband is a former state police investigator," she said. "Surely even you can see the difference."

"Dot, I can assure you that Suzanne is perfectly capable of handling herself in nearly every situation she runs into," Jake said proudly.

"Nine times out of ten, I heartily agree with you. It's that tenth time that always worries me," she admitted.

"Suzanne is nearly as resourceful as her mother, dear," Phillip said. It was good having him support me, too.

"I know that, but ultimately, she's just my baby girl. When I look at her, I see a skinny little girl with pigtails, freckles, and a missing front tooth," Momma said.

"Wow, that must be a stretch, even for you," I said. "Nobody's called me skinny since middle school."

"Stop fishing for compliments," Jake said with a smile. "I love the way you look."

"You have to say that. You're my husband," I told him.

"No, I have to say it because it's true," he corrected me.

Trish joined us at our table carrying two plates and looking a bit frazzled. "Hey, guys," she said when she realized that Jake and I had slipped in while she'd been otherwise occupied. "What can I get you?" she asked as she slid the meatloaf, mashed potatoes, and green beans in front of Momma and Phillip.

"Those look good," I said. "You're really hopping, aren't you?"

"What can I say? They come for the food, but they stay for my charm," she said with a tired smile.

"Maybe it's time to hire another high school girl to help out in the evenings," Momma suggested. "You're clearly running yourself ragged."

"I've thought about it, but just when I get them trained, they leave me. Do you remember what a nightmare Allison Jackson was? Besides, I hate paying people to stand around when we're not busy. I'm managing just fine."

"Trish, we're still out of tea over here," Mitch Jones said as he rattled his empty glass at Trish.

"You know where the pitchers are, Mitch. The clear one is unsweetened, and the golden one is sweetened. Help yourself."

"That's okay. I can wait," Mitch said sullenly.

"The last time I checked, your legs weren't broken," Trish said as she stood her ground and stared at him.

"Fine, but this is going to affect your tip," he threatened.

"I think I can find a way to live without your fifty cents," she said loudly enough for everyone to hear. "While you're at it, why don't you go ahead and make the rounds. You can refill everyone else while you're at it. Don't worry, you don't have to tip me at all tonight because of all of your hard work." Her grin said it all.

Mitch did as he was told without responding, and Momma said softly, "I can't believe you actually put him to work."

"Was it too much?" Trish asked her.

"Are you kidding? I think it's fabulous," she said.

Trish beamed from my mother's approval. Though I was her only child, many of the girls I'd grown up with had spent as much time at our cottage as they had at their own homes, and most of them felt as though Momma was theirs, too. In many ways, they were right, but I never got jealous. My mother had a heart big enough to love everyone, at least when she wasn't doing her best to poke at my buttons.

"What do you say, Jake? Two specials?" Trish asked him.

"Sounds good to me. Do you want me to clear some empty tables while I'm waiting?" he asked with a smile as he started to stand.

"Be careful what you're offering. I might just take you up on it," Trish said.

"Enough said," Jake replied as he grabbed a tub and began clearing tables.

"You don't have to do that," Trish protested. Was she actually blushing?

Jake just laughed. "The day I'm afraid of a little hard work is the day I hang it up as a human being." My husband worked with alacrity, doing the job with the same gusto with which he handled anything he tackled.

"Aren't you going to help him?" Momma asked me.

"It appears that he's doing just fine all by himself," I said, winking at Jake when I caught his eye.

He grinned and winked back. I knew he was enjoying himself, and I wasn't about to barge in on his fun. I half expected him to pick up an order pad and start waiting on customers, but he somehow managed to contain himself.

Jake returned to our table a few minutes later after washing his hands. Momma and Phillip were still eating, but our food hadn't arrived yet.

"Have fun?" I asked him.

"You know it," he said.

"What progress have you made on the attack?" Phillip asked between bites.

"Phillip," Momma said, warning him off the topic.

I knew he understood, but he wasn't going to just roll over for her. My mother needed someone strong in her life to stand up to her occasionally, and to my surprise, Phillip had become exactly that person. "Dot, it's a fair question. I used to be on the force, too."

"You don't need to remind me," Momma said.

"Admit it. You want to know, yourself," he tweaked his wife with a grin.

Momma tried to keep a stern face, but it quickly melted. "Of course I do," she said.

"So, spill the beans," Phillip prompted us.

"We have a ton of suspects, and a few thoughts as well," I said when Jake nodded to me to begin. "So far, we're looking at his sister, Noreen Walker, two ex-girlfriends, Vivian Reynolds and Gabby Williams, a former business partner, Bob Casto, an ally on the town council, Buford Wilkins, and a possible loan shark trying to make a point, though those last two aren't as obvious as the others."

"My, that's quite the list," Momma said.

"Tell them what else you suspect," Jake prodded me.

"About what?" I asked.

"The fact that Van may be hiding something," he prompted me.

"Oh, that. I got the distinct impression that Van's memory isn't as foggy as he'd like everyone to believe," I said.

"Why would he pretend to have amnesia?" Momma asked.

"Maybe he wants to settle the score himself," Phillip said. "That's what you're thinking, right?" he asked as he poked his fork at me.

"Right," I said, remembering that, all in all, my stepfather had been a fairly decent cop once upon a time.

"You left one name off your list though, didn't you?" Momma asked soberly.

"George didn't do it," I said firmly. I was a little surprised that my own mother thought the mayor might have done it.

"I want to believe that too, but we all know what a temper he has," she said as Trish arrived with our food. After she slid plates in front of us, she put our bill beside me. I glanced at it and saw that she hadn't charged us enough. "This isn't right."

Trish had clearly been hoping for me to comment. "Yes it is. I gave Jake the employee's discount." He started to dispute it, but Trish wouldn't allow it. "Not a word of protest, sir."

"I wasn't going to," he said, something that we all knew was a lie. "Thanks. I appreciate that."

"You're most welcome," she said as she hurried off to take another customer's money at the front.

As we ate, Momma and Phillip lingered to chat with us. Momma kept frowning about something though, and I finally had to ask what was going on with her. "What's wrong? Am I using the wrong fork or something?"

"There's only one at your plate, so I don't see how that's possible," she answered.

"Well, you're clearly staring at me for something. Go on. Spit it out."

"I may know a few things that might be pertinent to your case," Momma said. "Then again, they may both just be much ado about nothing."

"Why don't you let us decide? Don't hold back. At this point, we'll take any help we can get," I said.

After taking a deep breath, Momma lowered her voice as she said, "First of all, George isn't the only one Van Rayburn has argued with in public lately."

"Really?" I asked.

"Three days ago I overheard him quarreling with Buford about a parking space in front of his shop. Buford wanted the parking meter removed so his customers wouldn't have to pay to

park, and Van told him to stop wasting his time, that it wasn't
going to happen."

I frowned. "Is that really significant?"

"I know it sounds petty," Momma admitted, "but if there's
one thing I've learned over the years, it's that for some people,
the less power they have, the more they enjoy holding it over
others. Buford was clearly upset by Van's refusal, and they had
words."

"I get that, but was he angry enough to clobber him?" Jake
asked.

"Probably not," Momma said. "Then again, Vivian Reynolds
might have been, after what I saw."

Now it was getting interesting. "What did you see?"

"I saw Vivian was following Van down the street two days
ago," she said.

"How is that significant, Dot?" Phillip asked my mother
kindly.

"You should have seen the look in her eyes. There was a
hate there that startled me, but it wasn't just the stalking that
bothered me."

"What else happened?" Jake asked her.

"When Van paused to cross the street, I saw Vivian speed
up toward him. I thought for a moment she was going to push
him out into the road, but Van must have changed his mind
about crossing at the last second and started walking in another
direction. The thing is, there was a cement truck that would have
utterly destroyed Van if she'd gotten there in time and given him
a shove at precisely the right moment. It was the closest thing to
attempted murder I've ever witnessed in my life."

"Okay, that *is* significant," Phillip said. "What did you do?"

Momma looked down at her hands for a moment before
speaking. "I acted foolishly. Perhaps I've grown a little foolhardy
being around the three of you, but without giving it another

thought, I rushed over to Vivian and told her that I'd seen what she'd just tried to do, and that if anything happened to Van, I would make sure the police knew about it."

"Wow, that was absolutely reckless," I said with a smile. "I don't know that I've ever been prouder of you."

"It's not amusing, Suzanne," Phillip said, scolding me. "Dot, that was a dangerous thing to do."

"How did she react?" Jake asked her.

"That's the thing. She didn't seem all that upset by it all. The only thing she said was, 'You do what you have to do, and I'll do the same.'"

"That sounds like a threat to me," Phillip said as he reached for their check. "We need to go tell the chief."

"Phillip, I can't prove anything. As far as I know, no one else saw her actions, and she certainly didn't broadcast her threat to me loud enough for anyone else to overhear her."

"That doesn't matter. Until this thing is resolved, I'm not leaving your side," her husband said.

"As flattered as I am by the attention, it's not necessary." Momma looked at Jake and said, "Tell him he's overreacting."

"Actually, I think his reaction is perfectly reasonable," my husband said. "Vivian may or may not be a killer, but the woman is clearly off balance."

"Suzanne, be the lone voice of reason, would you?" Momma pled.

"I wish I could, but I'm with them."

Momma frowned at all three of us in turn, and then she stood. "Fine. Let's go find the police chief, Phillip."

"We'll touch base with you later," my stepfather said as they bustled out of the diner, throwing money at Trish on their way out.

We were still eating, so once they were gone, we finished our own meals.

Trish came by and asked, "Did you save room for dessert?"

"Thanks anyway, but we're stuffed," Jake said.

"Speak for yourself, John Alden," I said, remembering a line from our third-grade play. "What have you got?"

"Let's see. There's peanut butter pie, chocolate cake, and a triple threat brownie that's good enough to break your heart."

"All three sound great to me," I said. "You should offer a sampler platter."

I'd been joking, but clearly Trish took my suggestion to heart. "Not bad, Suzanne. I'll be right back," she said with a wicked grin.

"I was kidding," I said, but it was too late. She was already gone.

"I really was just teasing," I told Jake.

"Really? Does that mean that you're going to refuse samples of all three desserts when Trish comes back?"

"Well, I don't want to be rude," I said with a grin.

"I understand completely. In fact, I'd hate to be considered impolite myself, so in the spirit of being an all-around good guy, I'll help you."

"What happened to being too stuffed to eat another bite?"

"Suzanne, if I've learned anything from being married to you, it's that there's always room for a little treat." His grin was infectious.

Trish came back with two plates of samples, not one.

"We can share," I protested, though weakly at best. This way I'd be getting one all to myself.

"You're going to have to. The second one is for me. Mind if I join you?"

"We'd be delighted," Jake said.

I couldn't decide which treat I loved more, and everything was gone before I had a definitive answer. "You really should offer this on the menu."

"I will, but only when we have three equally worthy desserts," she said. "You're right, though. That was delicious." Instead of getting up and gathering our plates, Trish added, "You're looking into the attack on Van Rayburn, aren't you? Don't bother denying it. I've heard talk from a few folks that you're snooping around."

"That's interesting. Who exactly has been talking?" I asked her.

"Wes Granger was in here complaining about it an hour ago," Trish said. "I don't know why he was telling me. Did he honestly believe that I'd ever take sides against you?"

"He's just upset that we think Bob Casto might have had something to do with what happened to Van," I said.

"You're not the only one," Trish said.

"What do you mean?"

"Hey, I run the only diner in town. I hear things," she said.

"Anything that might help us in our investigation?" Jake asked her.

"So far it's all just been wild rumors and rampant speculation. In other words, my typical fare around here. There is one thing, though."

"What's that?" I asked.

"Gabby Williams wasn't happy about Van dumping her," Trish said softly. "I was doing inventory late last night when there was a knock at my door. It was nearly eleven, and I went to tell whoever was out there that we were closed, but then I saw that it was Gabby, and she'd obviously been crying. I must have sat with her four hours before I could get her settled down. I can't even count the number of times I almost fell asleep listening to her say what brutes men could be."

"That was so sweet of you," I said.

"Well, you know me. I never could stand seeing someone hurt," Trish explained.

"Are you sure about the timeline?" Jake asked.

"Positive. I kept staring at the clock the entire time. It felt more like four years, if you know what I mean."

"Gabby owes you a huge favor," Jake said. "You just gave her a solid alibi."

I'd been so wrapped up in Trish's tale that I'd forgotten the chief had given us the timeline of Van's night. Even if he never recovered his memory, or if he did and still refused to share it with us, Gabby was in the clear, and I was going to make sure that everyone knew it.

"I'm glad it was good for something," Trish said as she yawned. "I'm not sure I did her much good otherwise."

"You were there when she needed someone," I said. "Hey, that makes *you* her new best friend."

Trish shuddered at the very thought of it. "No, thanks. I'd hate to take your place." She stood, gathered up our dishes, and then we all made our way up front.

"You really don't have to give me a break on my meal," Jake said.

"I know I don't have to, but I want to."

"Then all I can say is thank you," Jake replied. I noticed that the tip he left more than made up for the discounted meal, and it was all I could do not to chuckle at my husband's handling of the situation.

We walked out of the diner, stuffed to capacity by the delicious dessert medley. I grabbed my husband's hand. "What's next?"

"I know we should probably be investigating, but why don't we go home instead and sit out on the porch swing and watch lightning bugs in the park?"

I laughed and gave him a big kiss. "There's nothing I'd like more."

"Besides, you have to get up to make donuts pretty early tomorrow," Jake said.

"Not tomorrow. Emma and Sharon are running the shop for the next few days. Like it or not, I'm all yours. You're stuck with me."

"I wouldn't call it being stuck," he said with a smile.

Sitting outside on our cottage's porch, even though it was summer, there was a slight chilly breeze in the evening air. I didn't mind, though. It gave us the opportunity to get out a light blanket and snuggle in the darkness, watching the fireflies dance among the trees. It was one of those moments I cherished above all others, a time of peace and total tranquility I could share with my husband.

Tomorrow would be soon enough to take up our investigation again.

Tonight was all ours, and I planned on relishing every last moment of it.

CHAPTER 12

"WHAT? YOU'RE KIDDING ME. OKAY. I'll tell her. Thanks."

Jake hung up the phone at breakfast the next morning and said, "Suzanne, you're not going to believe this."

"At this point, I'll believe practically anything," I said. I suddenly got an ache in the pit of my stomach. "Did someone take another run at Van?"

"No, but it did involve him. Bradley caught him trying to sneak out of his room at five a.m. this morning. The doctor took away his street clothes so he couldn't do it again."

"Where was he going?"

"He claimed to be out for a stroll, but it's pretty clear, isn't it? He was going after his attacker," Jake said.

"The man must have lost his mind when he got conked on the head."

"I don't know. If I were in his shoes, I might have done the same thing," Jake said softly.

"You'd try to get revenge?" His statement rattled me a little. After all, I had been under the impression that I was married to a law-and-order kind of guy, not some vigilante.

"I wouldn't attack whoever did it, but I would at least want the satisfaction of arresting him myself," Jake replied.

That answer I could live with. "Or her."

"Absolutely. Attempted murder is an equal-opportunity act," Jake said. "Let me wash these dishes, and we can be on our way."

"Let's stack them in the sink and save them for later," I said. "I don't think we should delay going to the hospital."

"Wow, you really are serious about this," Jake said with a slight smile.

"You know it."

As we drove to the hospital, I said, "I still think Van's crazy."

Jake just hummed a bit in response.

"He's not exactly equipped to tackle a would-be assassin."

Again, no real response from my husband.

"I'm going to cut my hair with a dull pair of scissors and dye whatever is left purple and blue."

"That would be nice," Jake said, still lost in thought. Ten seconds later, he asked loudly, "What did you just say?"

"Never mind. What deep thoughts are you pondering?"

Jake frowned for a moment before answering. "It was something you said earlier. It was kind of brilliant, actually."

"Why do you sound so surprised?" I asked him. "I say brilliant things all of the time. Just out of curiosity though, what did I say? I'd like to repeat it if I can."

"I'm not ready to share just yet. There are a few kinks I need to work out first."

I'd heard that tone of voice before. It wouldn't do me any good to push him until he was ready to share, even if I had had a part in his idea's formulation. "Okay by me. Van has got to tell us what's going on."

"I agree. How do we get him to do that, though?" Jake asked.

"We've tried being nice, and that didn't get us anywhere. Is there any leverage we can use on him to get him to tell us what he's remembered?"

"Wow, you're starting to sound more like a cop every day," Jake said.

"That didn't sound like a compliment to me."

"It wasn't," my husband answered. "Suzanne, leave the cynicism and the strong-arming to me. What you bring to the table is your neophyte enthusiasm to figure things out, and your way of getting people to open up to you. Those are two very valuable traits."

"Thanks, but sometimes people don't respond to those methods."

"Then you just have to find a way to approach them that makes them *want* to cooperate with you," Jake answered.

"Unfortunately, that's easier said than done," I answered.

"Hey, that's why you make the big bucks."

"I'm an amateur though, remember? By definition I'm unpaid."

"Well, at least you're not unappreciated," he offered.

"Yeah, I can live with that," I said as I pulled into the hospital parking lot.

Officer Bradley was on the door to Van's room.

"Don't tell me you were here all night," Jake said with a frown.

"No, I got my six hours of sleep. I got back here just in time to catch Mr. Rayburn trying to sneak out. He was dressed in his street clothes, but he was holding his shoes. The man's seen too many cartoons, if you ask me."

"Any idea where he was going?" Jake asked him.

"Not a clue. I don't buy his story that he just wanted to take a stroll, though." The officer's gaze narrowed for a second. "How did you already hear about it, anyway?"

"What can I say? Word spreads fast in a small town," Jake said.

I just nodded, and I was wondering who had tipped Jake off

to Van's attempted escape when I saw Penny Parsons, a nurse and a friend of mine, wink at Jake as she turned the corner. That rat had called my husband instead of me! I had to laugh. At least she'd phoned one of us.

"May we see him?"

"As long as he stays right where he is, you're welcome to go on in."

"Aren't you afraid one of us might be his attacker?" I asked him out of curiosity.

"The chief gave me permission to let you in. If you conk him again, it's on my boss's head, not mine."

Jake wasn't about to let it go that easily, though. "What exactly did you do to merit this duty two days in a row?"

"I'm not sure what you mean, sir," Officer Bradley said, suddenly being more formal than he'd been just before.

"You didn't volunteer for this assignment. I'll bet you that much."

The young cop just smiled. "I'm sure I don't know what you're talking about, sir."

Jake just laughed, which generated a chuckle from the police officer, too. "Got it."

Before we could go inside, I glanced quizzically at my husband, but he merely shook his head. If any explanation were coming, it would have to be later.

Right now we had to tackle the assault victim again.

"Going for a walk earlier, were we?" Jake asked the councilman as we entered the room.

"I was trying to, but that uniformed Neanderthal out front stopped me," Van said.

"I'd hardly call Officer Bradley that," I said. "How are

your doctors going to feel about you taking a stroll around the grounds?"

"I'm sure they'd be delighted. There's talk of discharging me later today, or tomorrow at the latest."

"Really? I'm surprised," Jake said. "Especially since you still haven't gotten your memory back. It *is* still gone, isn't it?"

"I don't recall a thing about the attack, if that's what you're asking," Van said in an extremely unbelievable way.

"Really? Are you still trying to sell that?" I asked him.

"I'm not trying to *sell* anything. It's the truth. I have a feeling that whoever did it isn't very likely to try it again," Van said.

"Were you born an idiot, or did you somehow come by it gradually over the years?" Jake asked him in a biting tone that surprised not only the patient but me as well.

"Watch it, buddy," Van said. "I'm a powerful man in these parts. You don't want to make me angry with you."

"I'm not too worried about it, especially since you're not going to be around long if you don't stop trying to act like some kind of one-man mob," Jake said. "I needed to get your attention, so I smacked you around a little."

"Well, you certainly got it, but you're not going to be happy getting it," Van said stiffly.

"Listen, and listen carefully. Whoever attacked you, whether you know their identity at this moment or not, isn't going to give up until you are in the ground," Jake said.

It was a side of my husband that I knew was there, but it still startled me when it bubbled to the surface. Jake was in full-on cop mode, and nothing would make him back off.

"Why would they care so much about hurting me?" Van asked, his tone decidedly less assured than it had been before.

"That's the thing. It's not about the first attack anymore," Jake explained to him in a nicer voice. "The attacker can't risk being exposed when and if you regain your memory. That makes whoever did it even more dangerous than before. Whatever their motivation to go after you was initially, it's been replaced by self-preservation, and I can't imagine anything good coming of it for you."

That seemed to rattle Van a little more. "Even if that's true, I can't stay under police protection around the clock. I have a life, you know."

"For how long, nobody knows," Jake said.

"So tell me, what do I do?" Van asked. His tough exterior was definitely cracking, and I had to wonder if he'd been telling the truth all along, that he had no clue who had attacked him in the first place.

"I've got some ideas, but you're going to have to follow my instructions to the letter if it's going to work. Can you do that?"

"If it means saving my own skin? You bet I can. What do I do?"

"I'll get back to you," Jake said. "There's just one thing I need to know, and I need the truth. Do you remember who assaulted you?"

"No," he said. "Sometimes I get a glimmer of an idea, but then it's gone as quickly as it came. If I knew, I'd tell you. Okay?"

Jake looked at me, and I nodded once. I actually believed Van. It had to be scary knowing that someone was out there ready to take another run at him after nearly succeeding on the first pass.

"Okay. Sit tight, and try not to make anyone else angry for the rest of the day. Can you do that?"

"I can try, but I won't make any promises," Van said. "Sorry, but that's the best you're going to get out of me."

"Then I suppose I'll have to take it," Jake said. "We'll be back later."

"I can't wait," Van said sarcastically.

Once we were out in the hallway and far enough away from Officer Bradley, I asked Jake, "When are you going to share your grand plan with me?"

"Soon. Very soon."

I knew that it was all I was going to get, so I decided not to argue the point.

I looked around the hallway and saw that it was virtually empty. "That's odd."

"What's that?" Jake asked as he scanned the halls himself.

"Where's Noreen? And how about Vivian? If nothing else, shouldn't Van's little toady Buford be around here someplace?"

Jake nodded. "I didn't even notice their absence."

"It's kind of tough to miss when no one is shouting," I said. "Maybe they knocked each other off."

"I'm not so sure you should be joking about that," Jake said.

"I know you're right, but I can't believe how adult women can behave so badly. If it weren't for Buford, we might have another assault on our hands."

"Don't sound so disappointed. You never know. The day's still young."

"Now who's acting all cynical and dark?" I asked him.

"It's okay if I do it," Jake answered. "It looks better on me."

"Maybe so, but we really need to figure this out, and soon."

"We're doing our best, not to mention the entire police force of April Springs. Somebody's going to break this case sooner or later," Jake said.

"I just hope it's sooner. I don't particularly like our councilman, but that doesn't mean I want to see anyone going after him again."

Jake walked back to the officer, who was watching us carefully, all the while pretending not to be. "I'm curious. Has Van's fan club been here today?"

Officer Bradley smiled. "They were here bright and early,

but Van ran them all off. He told them he needed his rest. You should have heard the grumbling. None of them wanted to leave his side. I don't know how he managed it, but those three are absolutely devoted to him."

"Are they gone for good?" I asked.

"I doubt it. I heard them promise to come back this evening, no matter how much Van might protest. I expect to see them about the time I get off shift at four thirty. If I'm lucky, anyway," he added with a slight smile.

After we stepped away again, I asked my husband, "What do you make of that?"

"Perhaps we can use the timing to our advantage," he said.

"Any idea how?" I asked.

"I'm working on it," was all that he'd tell me.

"So, what do we do in the meantime?"

"We need to get busy. There are other things we can do to help our investigation," Jake said as he started off down the hallway.

"Where exactly are we going?" I asked.

"I want to see if Bob Casto has gotten over his medications yet."

"Even if he has, how are we going to get past his entourage?"

"Trust me. I have a plan," Jake said.

As I followed him toward the businessman's room, I wondered what it was, but if I knew Jake, it was probably going to be a good one.

CHAPTER 13

A

S EXPECTED, THE CROWD WAS back in Bob Casto's room in full force. Jake didn't wait for any of them to say a word. "Somebody's been breaking into cars and trucks in the parking lot. If you have anything valuable in your vehicles, you might want to go check on them. The police are going around making random inspections to make sure that everything is safe."

It was actually brilliant. The ones who were innocent would naturally worry about the contents of their vehicles, while the ones who had anything shady in their cars or trucks would want to make sure the police didn't find anything they didn't want them to during their "random" searches.

The room couldn't have cleared out any quicker if I'd pulled the fire alarm.

Suddenly it was just Bob Casto, Jake, and me.

"Is any of that true?" Casto asked Jake once we were alone.

"All of it, at one time or another," Jake responded.

The businessman took that in, and after a moment, he said, "You went to some trouble to get us alone. What can I do for you?"

"Did you attack Van Rayburn?" Jake asked him bluntly.

"At least you're not beating around the bush. No, I didn't. Does that satisfy you?"

"As much as we'd like to take you at your word, you don't happen to have an alibi before you wrecked your truck, do you?"

Casto frowned. "When are you people going to leave me alone?"

"When you tell us the truth," Jake said.

Casto let out a deep sigh, and then he said, "Fine. I'll tell you, but if you repeat a word of it, I'll deny it. Do we understand each other?"

"Loud and clear," Jake said.

"I was with a woman," Casto said.

"Why the intrigue, then?" I asked him.

"She's married, and her husband has a pretty bad temper. I found that out firsthand."

"Tell us," Jake said.

Casto looked at me. "Her, too?"

"If you don't tell her now, I'll just tell her myself the second we leave here." I loved that Jake was willing to forego information just to protect my right to learn it at the same time that he did.

"Whatever. I was at Maureen Daniels's place last night when her husband came home unexpectedly. He caught us together, and he threatened to kill me. The man's been cheating on her for years, but when she slips up once, he goes all crazy."

I'd heard stories about Maureen, so I wasn't entirely sure that this was her first indiscretion with a man she wasn't married to, but there was no point in bringing it up.

"Anyway, he started waving a gun around, so naturally, I took off. Most men would have left it at that, but this maniac started after me in his truck, trying to drive me off the road. I was trying to get away from him when my truck spun out and I hit that tree."

"And he didn't even stop to help you when he saw you wreck?" I asked.

"I was lucky he didn't hang around and finish the job," Casto said. "The truth makes me look pretty corrupt, and I don't want my aunt to think badly of me, so I went along with Wes's deer-dodging story. Go on. Ask Maureen. Shoot, you can even ask her husband. I didn't go after Van. Why would I? How would I ever get my money back if I killed him? It just doesn't make good business sense. Now, you'd better get out of here before they come back. When they figure out that you lied to them, they aren't going to be too happy with you."

"I didn't lie entirely," Jake said. "I saw a patrolman out in the parking lot when we drove up, and I doubt your family is going to stop and quiz him about why he's there."

I hadn't seen anyone, but then again, Jake seemed to have a sixth sense when it came to spotting fellow officers.

Still, we did as Bob Casto suggested and left.

After all, if he was telling us the truth, and I suspected that he was, we'd just eliminated another extremely viable suspect.

That left us with Vivian, Buford, and Noreen.

Any one of them could have done it.

The question was, which one had? Were all three of them really as devoted to Van as they seemed?

Or was one of them sticking close just in case the councilman got his memory back so they could finish what they'd started if they had to?

As we headed back into town, I asked Jake, "Which of the three do you want to tackle first?"

"I was thinking about bracing Buford, then Noreen, and then Vivian," he admitted. "How does that sound to you?"

"It appears that you're starting with the least crazy one first and working your way up the ladder," I told him.

Jake frowned for a moment before he spoke. "I hadn't thought of it that way. What order would you like?"

"Oh, yours is fine," I said. "I was just teasing you."

"You make a good point, though. Okay, I've changed my

mind. Vivian is first, then we track down Noreen, and then we speak with Buford. Yes, I like that order better."

"Are you sure? I'm not trying to run this investigation, you know," I said.

"You're not. We're doing it together." Jake took a deep sigh, and then he admitted, "The truth is, most days I'd rather tackle an armed assailant than a scorned woman."

"Why is that?" I asked, curious about his rationale.

"At least the assailant's actions can be somewhat predicted," he said.

"Whereas a wronged lady's behavior can't?" I asked.

"I'm not being sexist, Suzanne. It's just been my experience that women *feel* more than men. You love deeper than we do, and when you feel betrayed, you have the capacity to hate that is startling to me, and I've seen a great deal as a cop."

"You're not talking about me specifically, are you?" I asked him with a grin.

"It was more of a universal 'you,'" he admitted.

"I can buy that," I said. "I've run into my fair share of crazy people in the past, but they haven't been limited specifically to one sex or the other."

"True enough. We should be watching our backs with everyone."

"That works for me," I said as I parked in front of Vivian's workplace in one of the strip malls on the way out of town. For the Birds sold wild bird food supplies, and unfortunately, I doubted that it would last the year. Vivian's boss and the store's owner, Jenny Preston, had decided to follow my lead, in a way. She'd taken her divorce settlement, and instead of buying a donut shop as I had, she'd opted to follow her own passion of feeding wild birds. Inside the small shop, there were not only dozens of exotic seeds and blends on display, but there were more flavors and variety of suet cakes than I could have imagined, feeders that ranged from the mundane to the exotic, and an unbelievable selection of books that covered everything from bird field identification to setting up backyard habitats.

As soon as Vivian saw us, she went into a defensive posture. "If you're here to talk about Van, I'm not interested."

"Maybe we're customers," I said.

"Seriously? You two are suddenly taking an interest in feeding wild birds?" Vivian asked with clear disdain.

"We live on the edge of the town park, so naturally we've thought about it from time to time," I said as I looked at a feeder based on the Cape Hatteras Lighthouse, with its diagonal black and white stripes. After I glanced at the price tag, I quickly vetoed that idea. Did people actually pay that much just to give food away to birds? "Do you have some kind of starter kit?"

"This one is nice," she said, showing us a multiple feeding station featuring sunflower seeds, thistle, and three different suet cakes. Did she work on commission or something? "I'm surprised you don't want to talk about Van. In fact, I'm kind of shocked you aren't at the hospital right now."

"I have to work if I expect to get paid," she said with a frown. "Besides, I've been asked to take a break from visiting Van."

"Was that the hospital's request?" I asked, knowing full well that Van had banished the lot of them himself.

"Does it matter? How is Van supposed to get better if we're all hovering around him like a pack of fleas? I'll go back later after I finish my shift. Now, about this feeder. It's got a deluxe delivery device for the seed, and the company claims that it's squirrel proof."

"I didn't think that was possible," Jake said.

"How do you even know that?" I asked him.

"Hey, I know things," he said with a grin.

"It's a tough uphill battle, and the squirrels eventually figure just about everything out, but this is a good place to start," Vivian said.

"I hope Van gets back on his feet soon," I said. It was my prompt for Jake to set the trap that we'd discussed earlier with Van Rayburn.

"We all do," Vivian said.

"There's a more practical reason than just wanting him back on his feet, though," Jake said. "Did you know his police protection is ending at five p.m. today? The chief says he can't afford to keep an officer at the door around the clock."

"I didn't think it was necessary in the first place," Vivian said stiffly. "No one's going to go to a hospital and attack a patient."

"I hope not," I said. On the spur of the moment, I decided to add, "The truth is, he's starting to get his memory back. The doctors believe it may all come flooding back to him at any moment. Isn't that wonderful?" It was worth a shot giving each of our suspects a little push in the right direction.

"It's excellent news," she said, though I couldn't tell if she was truly all that happy about hearing it.

I was about to add more when Jake said, "Thanks so much for your time. Suzanne, I need a little more time to think about feeding the birds before we take the leap. It's a big commitment, you know."

Vivian looked at him oddly. "What commitment? You fill the feeder when it's empty, and when you run out of supplies, you come back here to get more."

"We might be doing some traveling soon, though," I said, trying to back Jake's exit line. "Think how we'd feel if we had to leave town suddenly and the birds got hungry."

I knew it was lame, and Vivian was about to protest when Jake said, "Thanks again," and led me out of the store.

"Do you think your plan is going to actually work?" I asked Jake once we were outside again.

"If we don't stress the fact too hard that Van is going to be unguarded, it's worth a shot. After we move Van to another room and put a dummy in his place under the sheets, all we can do is wait."

"I'll try to be a little less enthusiastic about selling it with Buford and Noreen," I promised.

"Hey, I can't fault you for your passion," Jake replied.

Next up was Buford's fishing and fly-tying shop. At least it was nearby, located not fifty feet away from For the Birds. His shop was on the street instead of in the strip mall though, thus the troublesome parking meters he'd been trying to get removed. Hook, Line, and Sinker was another cute name, and I wondered if Donut Hearts was creative enough. Sure, it was a play on my last name, and I liked offering heart-shaped donuts occasionally, but maybe I should consider changing it to match so many other small businesses. I'd heard of other donut shops across the country named things like Glazed Over, Donut Addiction, and the Hole Donut, but somehow I just didn't think I could part with my name being in the title, so to speak. It was amazing what an ego could justify.

This shop was loaded with fishing paraphernalia, mounted fish, and more fishing-oriented gear than I thought was possible. My eyes kind of glazed over taking it all in, but Jake seemed delighted with the displays. Different strokes, I supposed.

"Hello," Buford greeted us when we walked in. Besides the three of us, the place was empty.

"How's business?" Jake asked cordially.

"It's just fin," he said nearly automatically.

I hoped we weren't in store for more fish puns.

"Looking for something in particular?" he asked us.

Jake was studying a rod, and from where I was standing, I could see that it was priced well into three figures. It was time to drop the façade that we were shopping before he walked out with something we really couldn't afford.

"Why aren't you with Van?" I asked.

"I saw him this morning," Buford said, "but just because he's laid up doesn't mean that the town of April Springs stops rolling. We have some important votes coming up soon, so we had to do a little strategic planning after breakfast."

"Was he really up to doing that?" I asked.

"He's getting better by the minute, if you ask me," Buford said. "Besides, the town needs a strong dialogue between opposing points of view, and until Van resumes his seat on the council, I'm stepping into the void. I know you are both fans of the mayor, but *everyone* needs to be kept in check."

"You sound as though you really enjoy politics," I said.

Buford shrugged before answering. "It's a diversion, nothing more than a hobby of mine. Fishing is my real passion. Did I ever tell you about the time I went deep-sea fishing off the coast of Florida and nearly snagged myself a..."

I didn't have any interest in hearing about his mythical conquest, no doubt elevated in the retelling to epic proportions.

"I'm sorry, but we're on a tight timetable. Jake is hosting his auction lunch today."

Buford nodded. "Stories from the force, and lunch catered by the hospital culinary genius. Yours was a hot ticket, my friend."

Jake replied, "You had quite a few bids yourself for fly-fishing in the mountains."

Buford frowned. "It's true enough, but it didn't turn out the way I'd expected."

"How so?" I asked, curious about who had won his prize.

"Betty Mathis bid on the package for her son, but he's not

going to be able to go, so Betty has decided that she wants to take his place. I'm not sure how it's going to go. We spoke briefly about the trip, and she told me she thought fish were slimy, and she wasn't touching any worms. We're fly fishing, for goodness sakes."

I didn't know what they used for bait, but I assumed flies, hence the name. How did they get the little buggers on the hook? Then Jake held up a brightly colored lure sporting tufts of feather and lots of color. "This one's a real beauty."

"That's my favorite fly. In fact, I tied it myself," Buford said proudly.

"Really?" Jake asked.

It was time once again to put the brakes on that particular conversation. "Did you hear that Van's losing his guard at five p.m. today? There's no budget for round-the-clock protection, even for the head councilman."

"We've got to find a way to increase our force's budget," Buford said. "I've been working on a proposal for years, but so far, it has been met with deaf ears. You'd think the mayor, a former police officer himself, would be onboard, but he claims there's just no money in the budget. Jake, you were a cop. Would you talk to him?"

"I could try, but George has a mind of his own," my husband opined.

"You don't have to tell me that," Buford said.

Building on what I'd told Vivian, I repeated the false news that I'd decided to spread. "There is some good news, though. Van said it's all starting to come back to him. He's hopeful that by this evening, he'll have his complete memory restored."

Unfortunately, we never got a chance to see Buford's reaction. All three of us turned as one as the door opened, and a man came in looking absolutely desperate. "Please. You've got to help me."

"What happened? Are you in trouble?" Jake asked as he

rushed to the man's side, ready to take over any emergency situation that came his way.

"You'd better believe it. My boss asked me to go fishing with him this weekend, and I need a complete rig, from top to bottom. We're talking clothes, equipment, guidebooks, the whole shebang."

Buford was practically salivating at the prospect of outfitting this man, and as a fellow small business owner, I couldn't blame him. One good customer could make or break a week, or even a month.

"If you'll excuse me," Buford told us even as he was turning toward the man. "My good fellow, let me assure you that you are in the best of hands. Now, let's get started."

The relief on the customer's face was palpable as we left.

"I knew you liked to fish occasionally," I told Jake once we were outside, "but I had no idea you were all that interested."

"Suzanne, I have to do *something* with my time," he said.

"What about your investigation business?" I asked, a fairly new thought he'd had.

"It turns out that most people only want private detectives for evidence in divorce cases, and I just don't have the stomach for it."

"Don't worry. Things will pick up," I said, doing my best to encourage him.

"We'll see. In the meantime, I need something to do with my time."

"I'm sure that between the two of us, we'll be able to come up with something," I said.

"That would be nice," was all that Jake would say.

He glanced at his watch. "I need to meet up with Barton in ten minutes."

"When is Ellie showing up?" I asked.

"In half an hour, but I promised the young chef I'd help on his end."

"You're not cooking, are you?" I asked, slightly aghast. My husband could grill out, and he could make chili, but that was about it.

"No, and there's no reason to sound so horrified, either. I'm going to set the table, fetch things for Barton, and generally try to make myself useful."

"Just don't be too accommodating, if you know what I mean," I said.

Jake wisely chose to ignore my comment. "What are you going to do for lunch?"

"I thought I'd pop in on Momma and Phillip," I said. "I don't feel like going to the Boxcar and explaining where you are a dozen times."

"I get that," he said, and then he kissed me soundly.

"Not that I'm complaining, but what was that for?"

"I just wanted to remind you that this is lunch, nothing more and nothing less. When it's over, I'm coming straight back to you."

"I didn't need the reminder, but that doesn't mean that I don't appreciate it," I said.

After he was gone, I thought about going on to see Noreen without him, but in the end I decided that it might be more prudent, for both our investigation and our marriage, if I waited for my husband.

Besides, my mother was always happy to feed me, even when I protested that I was full of whatever we were having at the time. I wasn't sure how pleasingly plump she wanted me, but if I kept going the way I was at the moment, I'd sail right past that designation into something a little less cutesy and a little closer to going up another size in clothes, something I swore that I would never do again.

I decided to give her a quick call and see if she was free.

CHAPTER 14

"HEY, MOMMA. ANY PLANS FOR lunch?"

"I'm just having leftovers," she said, "but you're more than welcome to join me."

My mother's leftovers were better than most meals I could get in a restaurant, and I always leapt at the chance to eat at her table. "That sounds awesome."

"Don't you even want to know what we're having?" she asked, the humor clear in her voice.

"If you made it the first time, I'll eat it the second. Phillip won't mind, will he?"

"Of course not. He loves having you here. That won't be an issue, though. My dear husband has buried himself at the library researching a new project."

"What is it this time?" I asked. My stepfather, once the chief of police for April Springs, had developed a real interest in unsolved crimes from the past, the farther back, the better, in some cases.

"He's researching the case of a woman who disappeared around the turn of the century. She was going to run off to be with her boyfriend, but apparently she never showed up at their rendezvous site."

"How does he even go about digging into something like that?"

"You'd be amazed by the eyewitness accounts printed in the newspapers of the time. He also digs and finds old journals and any other source of information he can lay his hands on. Actually, he's become quite adept at it."

"It doesn't surprise me to hear that at all." I'd been driving the entire time. I'd parked my Jeep in front of her cottage, and I'd walked up to the front door as we'd been chatting. Just for fun, I rang the doorbell, and I could hear it coming through the call.

"Hold on one second, dear. Someone's at the door."

She opened it and saw me standing there, waving like an idiot.

"Suzanne, honestly, must you continue to behave as though you were still a child?"

"Why wouldn't I?" I asked as I kept talking on the phone, even though we were now face to face. "That's what keeps me young."

Momma didn't play along though, as she disconnected the call from her end. "If it helps you to believe that, then by all means, continue to do so. Would you put that silly phone away and give your mother a proper hug?"

I did as she suggested. We shared a quick hug, me towering over her while at the same time feeling tiny in her presence. "Thanks for having me."

"You know that you are always welcome here," she said.

"So, what's on the menu?"

"A little bit of this and a smidgen of that," she said as I followed her to the kitchen. She'd already set two places at the small dinette where she and Phillip ate most of their meals, and the kitchen countertop sported a variety of containers.

"Oh, goody. I just love a buffet," I said enthusiastically as I grabbed a plate. In no particular order, I grabbed some lemon chicken slices, a spoonful of mashed potatoes, a dash of green beans, a little meatloaf, and some Brussels sprouts and cheese sauce.

"Let me heat that up for you," she said.

"I can manage it," I protested, but she took the plate from

me anyway. Sometimes my mother just couldn't help mothering me, no matter how old I got.

"I have a new way to do it," she said as she tore off a section of plastic wrap and put it over my plate. "This steams the food as it microwaves," she said.

"Sounds good to me. I'll get the drinks. What would you like?"

"There's milk in the fridge, but I just made some fresh lemonade. It's just not summer without it, you know?"

"You don't have to convince me. You raised me on the stuff, remember?"

"I'm not likely to forget," she said as the microwave oven chimed. She touched the plastic lightly and then added another thirty seconds to the timer. Once it was ready, she peeled the plastic back and put my plate down. "Now don't wait on me. It's best when it's hot."

"I'll take my chances," I said as I poured us two glasses of lemonade and put them at our place settings.

"Very well," Momma said, quickly making up a plate for herself and repeating the process she'd just used with mine.

After I said the childhood grace I'd learned long ago, we dug in.

"This is amazing," I said as I started with a bite of meatloaf. "No matter how hard I try, I never seem to be able to make mine as good as yours is. What's your secret? And don't say love. I've looked for that on the store shelves, but they always seem to be out."

"I like to add a little barbeque sauce to the mix," she admitted.

That was the taste I hadn't been able to identify. "And you're just telling me this now why, exactly?"

"It's a family secret," she said with a grin.

"Some secret," I said with a smile in return. "I'll try it myself the next time I make meatloaf. Seriously though, why haven't you told me up until now?"

"You'll think I'm just being a foolish old woman," she said softly.

"I promise I won't," I answered, more curious now than ever.

"I was afraid that if you knew how to make it yourself, you wouldn't come around as often for mine," she admitted timidly.

I stood up and hugged her. "Momma, as much as I love all of your cooking, you are the real draw, not the menu."

"Thank you for that," she said with a slight smile. "Now eat before it gets cold." Wow, it hadn't taken her long to go into full-on Mom mode that time.

As we ate, she asked, "How's Van doing?"

"He's clearly feeling better, but he still claims he doesn't know who attacked him."

"Have you and Jake uncovered anything new yet?" she asked with real interest. Since my mother had participated in one of my investigations herself, she'd become quite interested in the cases I took on from time to time.

"More than I could have imagined, but we're still not all that close to figuring out who did it," I said. "Actually, that's not true. We have managed to eliminate Bob Casto as a suspect, and Gabby Williams, as well."

"That sounds to me as though you're making progress, though I can't imagine Gabby clubbing Van from behind. In the front, face to face, maybe, but not from the rear. That leaves Vivian, Noreen, and Buford, doesn't it?"

"Yes, but we're having a hard time figuring out which one of them it might be," I said. "Jake has an idea we're going to try out this evening."

"Is it risky?" Momma asked. Of course she'd go straight to that.

"Not unless you're a dummy," I said.

She frowned a moment before speaking. "Suzanne, you know

I don't like you referring to people that way. It's unkind, and what's more, it's beneath you."

"Momma, I'm talking about an actual dummy, like the kind they use for CPR classes." Jake had arranged to borrow one after chatting with Penny. It appeared that she was becoming better friends with my husband than she had ever been with me. Did that bear watching, or was I just being paranoid again? Probably the latter. After all, if I was going to be jealous of someone, there was no doubt in my mind that Ellie deserved my full consideration. Thinking of my husband having lunch with that siren must have caused me to frown for a moment. Most folks would have probably missed it, but my mother was, if anything, not most people.

"Why the sudden frown?" she asked.

"Jake is having lunch with Ellie Nolan even as we speak," I told her.

"Suzanne, you have nothing to be jealous of. The woman exists solely on the surface."

"Just because she's a gym rat?" I asked.

"Of course not. I have many friends who love to work out. Ellie is what she is for many reasons, but none of them have to do with her chosen occupation."

"Momma, you've seen her. I'd be delusional not to be at least a little concerned."

"Your husband loves you, dear."

"I know that," I said, not at all proud of my reaction to Ellie going out of her way to share a meal with my husband. I was just as frail and unsure of myself as the next gal at times, though, and I wasn't quite sure why I was being so hard on myself.

"Could it be because Max cheated on you with a woman of much the same type?" Momma asked softly.

My fork hovered in the air as though I'd suddenly lost control of my hand. "Of course that's it. Why didn't I see it before?" My first husband had betrayed me with a woman who worked at the beauty parlor, and the more I thought about it, the more I realized just how much Darlene and Ellie had in common, at least superficially. "I owe my husband an apology, don't I?" I asked her.

"It never hurts to give one when it's needed," she said. "At least now that you're aware of it, you won't make matters worse."

"If only you were right," I said with a sigh.

"Suzanne," she said, using my name to scold me as she had done countless times in our past.

"Momma," I replied, using the same emphasis she just had.

We both stared at each other for a split second, and then we burst out laughing.

Jake came in a little later, and I felt much better about the situation. Shoot, I didn't even check him for lipstick.

"So, how was it?" I asked.

"Unbearable," Jake said as he joined us in the living room. Momma and I had done the dishes together side by side, just like in the old days, despite the fact that she owned a dishwasher. I didn't mind. It was a way to share the closeness that I cherished.

"How so? Surely the food was good," Momma said. She too was a big fan of Barton's cooking.

"The meal was amazing," Jake replied. "The company not so much."

"What happened? Did she throw herself at you?" I asked, trying to smile as I said it to take the sting out of my inquiry.

"Hardly. She barely managed to utter ten words to me the entire time. It quickly became apparent why she bid on my auction entry. It had less to do with my stories and more to do with the new chef."

"That's a change for her, isn't it?" I asked. Since Ellie seemed to like only older men in the past, I'd just naturally assumed that she'd go after my husband.

"It appears to be," Jake said.

"How did Barton react to the attention?"

Jake grinned for a moment before speaking. "I'm not quite sure he even realized that she was throwing herself at him. That boy has a singular focus when it comes to cooking, and I have a feeling that he's so smitten with Emma that he literally does not notice other women."

"How did Ellie take that?" I asked, not even trying to hide my smile now.

"She was clearly baffled at first, but then, as she kept getting more and more obvious about making a play for him, she started to get angry. After she left us abruptly, Barton asked me if there'd been anything wrong with the food. When I assured him that it had been excellent, he seemed even more puzzled than he had been before."

"I would have paid good money to witness that," Momma said. "I won't even try to feed you, Jake. I won't have my food compared to his."

"You're each supreme chefs in your own way," Jake said.

"When did you get to be such a smooth talker?" Momma asked him, clearly delighted by the comparison.

"Suzanne has been working on me," Jake admitted.

"Well done, Suzanne. When you're finished with him, perhaps you can take a run at Phillip," she said with a smile.

"Are we *ever* really done fixing the men we marry?" I asked with a laugh.

"Hey, I'm standing right here. You can both see me, right?" Jake asked with a smile.

I kissed him soundly, and then I gave Momma a quick buss as well. "Thanks for lunch, and the company. Both were outstanding."

She seemed to relish the compliments. "You are welcome any time." After we hugged, she added, "You are as well, Jake."

"Be careful about those invitations," he said with a grin. "I might just take you up on them."

"Nothing would delight me more," Momma said, and it was clear that she meant every word of it.

I followed Jake back to our cottage so he could drop off his truck, and then it was time to track Noreen Walker down and set the last bit of our trap.

I couldn't wait until the evening to see if we actually caught anything in it.

CHAPTER 15

"NOREEN, WE CAN SEE YOU in there," I said as I rang her doorbell again. She was living in an apartment complex on the other side of town. The place was full of young couples, singles, and other older folks, clearly none of them all that well off financially. We'd rung the bell, knocked, and rung it again, but she had so far refused to answer our summons. Jake had peeked in through a slit in the curtains, and he'd spotted her hiding behind a sofa. "It's Jake and Suzanne. We just want to talk to you."

I could hear some movement inside, due more to the flimsy construction than Noreen's heavy footsteps. "What do you want?" she asked, still not opening the door.

"Are you seriously not going to talk to us face to face?" I asked her.

"I'm not presentable," she said.

I wasn't sure exactly what that meant. Maybe she was doing us a favor by not opening the door after all. "Fine. We just wanted to give you an update on your brother."

That got her attention. The door opened, though she kept the chain lock in place, allowing us only a sliver of view. From what I could see, Noreen was in a ratty old bathrobe, and her hair was in curlers. I'd seen worse, but not by a whole lot. "What is it? Has he taken a turn for the worse? Is he unconscious again?"

Was that a hopeful tone in her voice? I honestly couldn't tell.

"Quite the opposite. As a matter of fact, he seems better. The police are ending their guard on his door at five today," I said.

"They are what? But he's still in danger!" She sounded like a concerned sister. There was only one problem. She'd hesitated for a moment before reacting. Was she just that slow, or was her concern just contrived? I honestly couldn't tell.

"It is what it is. We spoke with him earlier, and he has a hunch his memory will be coming back soon. He's already catching bits and pieces, so it won't be long until he remembers who attacked him."

"That's good news," she said. "Now if you'll excuse me, I have to continue getting ready."

"Are you going back to pay him a visit?" I asked.

"No, he was most specific about that. I'm going to see a man in Union Square about selling my mother's brooch, if you must know. It's a silly little frill, and I have no real need for it anymore." She moved her hand to her robe, and I caught a glimpse of the piece of jewelry in question, proudly pinned to her robe. She stroked it as though it were a sacred talisman, and I knew that she hated the prospect of giving it up. I hoped that I never found myself in such dire straits that I had to sell something dear that had once belonged to my mother. It was a sobering thought.

Noreen closed the door quite abruptly in our faces.

"What now?" I asked Jake, who'd been carefully listening in to our conversation.

"There's not a great deal we can do but wait at this point," he said. "I don't know about you, but I could use a nap. Interested?"

"I rarely pass up the opportunity for a little siesta," I said, still stuffed from the wonderful lunch with Momma.

"Then it's a date," Jake said.

We never made it back home, though.

At least not in time to take a nap.

There was something much more pressing that we had to deal with.

One of our friends was in trouble, and there was never any doubt in either of our minds that we were going to help.

As we drove past, the doors to Two Cows and a Moose were standing wide open, and there was a chain of people flooding into Emily Hargraves's newsstand.

I pulled into the closest spot. "Something's wrong, Jake."

"Let's go see if we can help," he said without hesitation, the promised nap now forgotten.

We walked into pandemonium. There was a good two inches of water on the floor, and the tide was coming dangerously close to the first level of magazines, books, and periodicals Emily sold.

"What happened?" I asked Emily, "and what can we do to help?"

"The water heater exploded!" Emily said. "We need to shut the water off, but no one seems to be able to find the valve."

At that moment, George Morris came out of a small closet I'd noticed before but never knew what it contained. His shirt and hair were soaked, and so were his shoes and the bottoms of his pants. It didn't explain his triumphant expression. "Found it!" he shouted. "It was behind a false wall panel." He seemed to notice us for the first time. "Coming to lend a hand?"

"You know it," I said. "What can we do, Emily?"

"Start boxing things up and taking them out onto the sidewalk. The water level isn't rising anymore, but this dampness could still ruin everything."

"Let me round up some guys and gals with trucks," George said as he pulled out his phone. "We can set you up in one corner of town hall. Shoot, you can even run your store from there until this all gets fixed."

"Can you actually do that, let a business be run on April Springs property?"

"Who's going to stop me? If anybody tries, I'll be ready for them. I've been itching for a good fight, and this is just the ticket."

The last thing the mayor needed was another fight on his hands. After a brief whispered conversation with Jake, I said, "Emily, I've still got the building Dad left me. Use that. That way there won't be any problems."

"I couldn't put you out, Jake," she said. "You're using the space yourself now, right?"

"It's all yours," Jake said. "I can use the small room in the back, and you can have the main space. It's not as much square footage as you're used to here, but it should do in a pinch."

"I can't thank you both enough," she said.

"Then it's settled," George said. "I'll get things started from my end."

"I'll go unlock the building and move a few things around," Jake volunteered.

"This is so sweet of you, Suzanne," Emily said with tears in her eyes after the two men were gone. "I don't know how to thank you enough. Everyone is being so kind."

"We're your friends, Emily. We stick together." I noticed her mascots, Cow, Spots, and Moose, three stuffed animals she'd had since childhood, sitting on their shelf high above the store. "Please tell me you didn't take the time to change their outfits when this place started flooding."

She laughed despite the calamity she'd nearly suffered. The three stuffed animals were all dressed in identical bright-yellow raincoats, matching hats, and colorful boots. As I got closer, I saw that Cow and Spots had little cows on their boots, while Moose's foot attire sported images of his own kind. "They were like that for April Showers, but so many loved the outfits I decided to keep them on until it was time for their Uncle Sam uniforms again for July Fourth."

"We'll have to put a shelf in for them in the new place," I said.

"You don't have to go to that much trouble," she protested.

"It's no trouble at all," I said.

Max came in, soaking wet. "Sorry. I couldn't find a plumber anywhere."

"George shut the water off," she explained after they kissed briefly. I had no problem with my ex-husband dating a dear friend. Maybe it was because I was happily married myself, or it could have been because Max had done some growing up over the years. Either way, I was glad they had each other in their lives.

"Suzanne is letting me use her building over on Viewmont Avenue," Emily explained.

"That's really generous of you," Max said. "Thanks."

"Happy to do it," I said. "Now, where can we find more boxes?"

"Did someone say they needed boxes?" Momma asked as she and Phillip came in carrying loads of unfolded ones. "We cleaned out the hardware store."

"Then let's get busy," Max said.

Momma was a little cool toward my ex-husband, but considering how she'd once felt about him, it was an absolutely glowing reception.

"Thank you, ma'am."

"I'd do anything for Emily," she said, and then she even managed to offer him a brief smile.

It was the warmest I'd seen her toward him since we'd broken up.

"Your daughter has been gracious enough to loan me her building on Viewmont," Emily said as my assistant, Emma, and her mother, Sharon, walked in. "Isn't that fabulous?"

"Suzanne has a good heart," Momma said, smiling at me in approval. It didn't matter how old I got, I still loved it when she was proud of me.

Three hours later, we were just about finished with the move. Phillip and Jake had even installed a new shelf for the three stuffed animals, who looked bemused by the entire situation.

As I handed Emma the keys, I said, "Stay as long as you need to, okay?"

"I'm going to pay you rent. I insist, so don't make me force you to take my money," she said grimly.

"Fine. We'll work something out," I said, having expected that reaction from the beginning.

"I'm talking about fair market value, Suzanne. I mean it."

She must have known that I was going to ask for a token payment, but she had me now. "Okay, but I might donate it to a good cause. Would that be okay with you?"

"Of course. Where did you have in mind?"

"The soup kitchen could still use some contributions, even after the auction," I said.

"That's perfect," she answered.

Jake approached and tapped my shoulder. "Sorry to interrupt, but we need to go, Suzanne."

I'd completely lost all track of time. If we were going to get Van set up somewhere else and stage his room, we'd have to get going.

I felt my heart race as we hurried toward my Jeep.

With any luck, before too much longer, we just might finally discover who had attacked Van Rayburn and left him for dead.

CHAPTER 16

P ENNY MET US IN THE hallway outside Van's room. "Is he still in there?" Jake asked her.

"No. We moved him to 207," she confided in a near whisper, "but as far as everyone here is concerned, he's officially still in there."

"I can't thank you enough for helping us, Penny," I told her.

"It's the least I can do after what Jake did for my cousin," she said.

"What did you do?" I asked him. Why hadn't I heard about it if Jake had helped someone out?

"It was nothing," my husband said, clearly trying to brush my question off.

Penny wasn't about to allow that, though. "Don't kid yourself. A good word from you went a long way with the judge. My entire family is in your debt. Taking the time to meet with Taylor, and then standing up for him, was above and beyond the call of duty."

I was really intrigued now. "Jake, tell me what happened."

He looked almost embarrassed to recount what he'd done, but he was on the spot now. "Penny asked me if I'd look into Taylor's arrest. It didn't take long to see that he was just in the wrong place at the wrong time, but his public defender wasn't very adept. I spoke with the arresting officer, and he admitted that he might have been a little too enthusiastic arresting the boy. We spoke to the judge together, and he dismissed the charges. The entire thing took two hours. You were at work, so there really wasn't that much to tell."

I knew that my husband had a kind heart, and though he could be tough when it was needed, he also had a kindness in him that I cherished. It certainly went a long way toward explaining how much Penny had been cooperating with us lately.

"We'll never forget your kindness," Penny said.

Jake clearly wanted to move past the discussion. "Did you set things up like we discussed?"

"Even better. See for yourself," she said with a grin.

Jake and I stepped into the room, which had been darkened to give only a slight illumination. It appeared that someone was in the bed sleeping, even though I knew otherwise.

"That's amazing," I said, as a soft snore began to fill the room. "How did you do that?"

"My uncle is an electronics nut. When I approached him about making this more realistic, he set up a switch on the door. After three seconds, a recording of him snoring starts playing. It lasts about five minutes. Will that be long enough?"

"It's perfect," Jake said, and then, to my surprise, the body shifted slightly under the sheet.

"Are you sure no one's there?" I asked.

She laughed. "Uncle Tim got carried away. He put some kind of widget under the dummy's chest to make it move sporadically. It's cool, isn't it?"

"Amazing," I said. "Can you reset it?"

After she did as I asked, she said, "The bathroom is the best place to hide. If you leave the door cracked, you can see whoever comes in without being spotted yourself. Do you really think it's going to work?"

"It's a coin toss, but at the moment, it's the best idea we could come up with," Jake said. "Thanks again for setting this up."

"This doesn't even begin to pay the interest on the debt we owe you," Penny said, and then she was gone.

"Wow, you really saved the day with her family, didn't you?" I asked softly once we were ensconced in the bathroom. "Why didn't you tell me about it?"

"I didn't want to seem as though I was bragging," Jake said. "It really wasn't all that much."

"It doesn't sound that way to me."

I kissed him soundly, and after a moment, he asked, "What was that for?"

"I figured you deserved some kind of reward for being gallant," I said. "Is that okay with you?"

"If I'd known I'd get that kind of attention from you, I would have told you sooner myself," he said with a grin.

I had to stifle my laugh, just in case someone was lurking outside the room.

Twenty minutes later, I was bored to tears, but Jake seemed fine. "How do you do it?"

"Do what?" he whispered, his gaze never leaving the hospital room door.

"I'm about to climb the walls, but you seem as though you could do this well into the night."

"Suzanne, I've been on so many stakeouts I've lost count. There are ways to pass the time, mostly rehashing old memories and analyzing past decisions, things like that, that keep the mind occupied."

"That sounds even worse than just standing here waiting for someone to show up," I admitted.

"You get used to it," he said softly, just as the door began to show a sliver of light. "Shhh."

I peeked out and saw the sliver widen, and a moment later, I knew who had come calling on Van.

There was enough light to see Vivian clearly, and she had a scowl on her face as the dummy appeared to start snoring. She didn't say a word as she crept toward the bed.

Scanning the room, Vivian spotted a pillow on the chair beside the dummy. She nearly jumped out of her skin when it moved, but after thirty seconds, when it remained still, she grabbed the pillow and started toward the dummy.

She was poised just above its head when Jake reached out and flipped on the light switch.

Vivian couldn't have looked more surprised if the dummy had leapt up and shouted, "Surprise!"

"Stop right there," Jake said as he hurried toward her, his weapon drawn. How had I missed the fact that he'd been armed?

"What are you doing lurking in there?" she asked as the pillow slipped from her hands onto the floor.

"You were about to smother him, weren't you?" I asked.

"No! Of course not!" Her denial seemed a little too strong to me, and a bit too late to feel real.

"Then what were you going to do with that pillow?" Jake asked her.

"If you'll put that weapon down, I'll tell you," she protested.

"Thanks for the invitation, but I believe I'll keep it right where it is for the moment. Now, about that pillow."

"I was going to climb into the bed beside him," she said. "Is there a law against that?"

"It didn't look like that to us," Jake said. He pulled out his cell phone with his free hand, made a call, and then we both heard him ask, "Are you still in the hospital? Suzanne and I were right. Vivian just tried to smother the CPR dummy." After Jake put his phone away, he said, "He'll be right here."

"What do you mean, dummy?" Vivian asked, staring down at the body under the sheet.

I reached down and slipped the sheet off the CPR dummy, and Vivian gasped when she realized that it wasn't Van. "You tricked me!"

"A good thing, too, or Van might not have been so lucky this time. Why did you try to kill him, Vivian?"

"I did no such thing!"

"Don't bother denying it," I said. "We both saw you."

Before she could say another word, the chief burst into the room. "Good work, you two."

Only then did Jake lower his weapon. "She was about to try to suffocate him when we stopped her."

"I told you, I was just climbing into bed with him! You have all gone insane!" The last bit was shouted, and I could swear I saw a hint of madness in her eyes.

"Why don't we go back to my office and talk about it?" the chief asked as he reached for Vivian's arm.

"You're not going to handcuff me, are you? I hate feeling restrained." There was a whimpering quality to her voice that made me feel sorry for her, at least until I remembered what she'd just tried to do.

"Then you're going to really hate the holding cell," Chief Grant said. As he led her out, he asked, "Jake, would you mind joining me? I'd like to get your statement, and then maybe you could sit in on the interrogation."

I knew there was nothing my husband would like more, but he still turned to me and asked, "Do you mind?"

It was all I could do not to smile. "You go on. I'll catch up with you later."

"Thanks," he said, and then the two men escorted Vivian out of the room.

Penny came in two seconds later. "Is it all over?"

"It seems to be," I said. "Thanks again for your help. Do you need any help putting this back to normal?"

"No, I've got it. It was kind of fun."

"I guess," I said, remembering the crazed look in Vivian's eyes. There had been nothing entertaining about that.

"So, what now?" she asked me.

"I thought I'd go tell Van what happened," I said. "He has a right to know who tried to attack him again."

"I know if it were me, I'd want to know," she said.

"You said Room 207, right?"

"Right," she said.

I walked down the hallway to Van's room.

He was sitting up in bed doing a crossword puzzle, in pen, no less.

"It's all over," I said when he looked up.

"Who was it?" he asked. "I still don't have a clue who attacked me at my place."

"Vivian Reynolds just tried to smother a CPR dummy," I said.

Van took that in, and then he frowned as he let out a heavy sigh. "I wish I could tell you that I'm surprised by that, but I'm not. She always was a little bit crazy."

"Then why did you go out with her in the first place?" It was a question I often wondered about, why men dated certain women they knew were unstable.

"What can I say? She was lively, spontaneous, and unpredictable," he said. "At first, it's what attracted me to her, but in the end, it's what made me go for Gabby instead."

Gabby Williams could be described as many things, but never those three adjectives, at least not in my mind.

"Are you having second thoughts about dumping her?" I asked him.

Van looked saddened by the thought. "She'd never take me back after dumping her like that."

"I don't know. I wouldn't write her off just yet," I said.

"Do you think I still have a chance?" he asked.

"Look at it this way. What do you have to lose?"

For the first time in days, Van actually seemed hopeful.

It lasted less than three seconds, though.

Someone else, the real attempted killer, I suddenly knew, destroyed that by coming into the hospital room wielding a long and deadly-looking knife held tightly in a latex-gloved hand.

Apparently Jake and I had caught the wrong assailant in our trap.

CHAPTER 17

"BUFORD, WHAT ARE YOU DOING here?" Van asked his second-in-command on the town council as the man waved the knife menacingly in our direction.

"I followed Suzanne after her husband and the police chief took Vivian away. I must admit, it was a good trap you set. I almost fell for it myself when Vivian burst in before I could manage it myself."

"*You* attacked me? Why?" Van asked, clearly bewildered by the identity of his real assailant.

"Do you really even have to ask? You were always putting me in my place, making sure that I knew that *you* were the real power on the town council. I got sick of being bullied, so I decided to take matters into my own hands."

"I never bullied you," Van protested.

"Please. Between you and the mayor, I knew that I'd never get control if I didn't take matters into my own hands."

"That's why you used the trophy," I said as it all suddenly began to make twisted sense. "You decided to kill Van and frame the mayor for it. With them both out of the picture, it would be easy enough to step into the void left behind."

"You did this for our *jobs?*" Van asked incredulously. "I make nine thousand dollars a year, and the mayor makes a measly twelve grand."

"It was never about the money," Buford protested. "It's the

power that counts. I figured the world, and April Springs, were better off without you two running things around here."

Van's face suddenly lightened. "It *was* you! I remember everything now!"

"Too little, too late, though," Buford said with a nasty little smile.

"How are you going to frame the mayor for this?" I asked, searching desperately for something to use as a weapon to fight back with. Unfortunately, the room was rather stark. There was a pillow and a folded blanket nearby, but I wasn't sure how I could use either one of them to overpower the madman.

"This knife belongs to the mayor," he said happily.

"Why would he attack me, though? He's my friend," I said, easing toward the pillow. Maybe I could use it to deflect a knife thrust. Then again, the blade appeared to be sharp enough to penetrate it easily, but what choice did I have?

Fighting back was in all ways better than dying passively.

I might not survive the attack, but I was at least going to make him earn it. My plan, if I didn't make it, was to at least scratch his face. If I could get some of his DNA under my fingernails, my death wouldn't go unavenged, and he'd be marked publicly with my brand.

My husband would never allow him to go free.

I needed to distract Buford before I could rush him, though. "You were there when Gabby showed up, weren't you?" I asked him.

"I was nearly ready to kill them both, but fortunately, at least for her sake, Van never mentioned me. He was in too big a hurry to brush her off. I waited until I was sure she was gone, and then I hit Van with everything I had." He turned to his attack victim as he added reprovingly, "I was sure you were dead! How you managed to hang on, let alone crawl to the door, was astounding." He looked at me in disgust. "If you and the mayor hadn't found him when you did, there's no way he could have held on until morning. In a way, you've brought this on yourself, Suzanne."

I could see Buford tense up, but I had to delay him for another second so I could finalize my sketchy plan of attack. "That's why you've been hovering around here since Van checked in. You were waiting to see if he'd regain his memory."

"Of course that's why. Do you think I did it because I was devoted to the man? Please. Don't be ridiculous. When you told me his memory was starting to come back, I knew that I had to act."

"It was all a lie, you know," I said, trying to get him angry. It was a dangerous move, but since he was going to kill me anyway, what did I have to lose? If I could somehow enrage him, maybe he'd get sloppy, and I'd have a chance. "Even a fool should have seen right through it."

"Are you calling me a fool?" Buford asked, his hand tightening on the knife handle.

"If the shoe fits," I said with as much derision as I could muster.

"Suzanne," Van said, clearly trying to warn me off, but I was committed.

"Come on, Van. Couldn't you do better than *him*? Did you really think he was worthy of being your right hand on the council? He can't even do this right."

I glanced at Buford and saw that he was livid with anger.

"You're going to pay for that!"

He was about to move when the hospital door room began to open! Was I about to get reinforcements?

"Van? Are you in here?" Noreen asked.

She wasn't going to be of any help, but she'd managed to do something anyway.

The moment Buford turned to her, I grabbed the pillow and swung it at Buford's hand holding the knife. It was a weak weapon, but it managed to catch him off guard anyway. He didn't drop the knife, but he did take a step backward and lower it.

It was all that I needed. I tackled him, wrapping my arms around his so that he couldn't stab anyone. He struggled against my grip, and in an instant, I could feel that I was losing control!

"Get help!" I shouted at Noreen.

She stood there paralyzed, but thank goodness Van didn't. The moment I'd grabbed Buford, Van had leapt from the bed and thrown himself into the fray. No matter what I thought about him, I had to give him credit. He acted swiftly and decisively, coming to my aid, and that got him a great many points in my book.

"Go, Noreen!" he shouted at his sister, and that finally got her attention.

Buford was screaming at both of us now, writhing and twisting as though he were some kind of snake, but we didn't let go. I'd been stabbed not that long ago, and I was in no hurry to repeat the experience.

Thank goodness I didn't have to.

Twenty seconds later, the same armed security guard I'd seen earlier showed up, and once he had his weapon trained on Buford's midsection, the man collapsed as though he were made of straw.

"Thanks for helping out," I told Van.

"Don't thank me. If you hadn't jumped him, we'd both be dead right now. I kept hitting the call button, but it must not be working."

"At least Noreen came in when she did," I said, trying to catch my breath.

"It was still too close for my taste," he said. "I don't know how you do it, Suzanne."

"What, make donuts every day?" I asked him with a grin.

"That too, but I was talking about investigating crimes like you do. Speaking of donuts, you still owe me a lesson."

"And the mayor, as well. Do you think this will help you two get along better in the future?"

"Probably not," Van said with a grin.

Jake and the police chief burst into the room, and my husband wrapped me up in his arms. "We just heard what happened." The chief cuffed Buford and led him out. Clearly there was no fight left in the man.

"Everything's okay," I said, offering him comfort, despite the fact that I'd been the one who'd recently been attacked. "Van really stepped up."

"Don't give me too much credit. It was mostly just self-preservation," the councilman said, getting some of his bravado back.

Jake wouldn't hear of it, though. He released me and approached Van with his hand extended. "I owe you, sir."

"It's okay," Van said.

"I mean what I say," Jake replied. "I am in your debt. Any time you need me, day or night, I'll be there."

Van nodded, and then Jake came back to me. "Let's get you out of here, okay?"

"That sounds like a good plan to me," I said, happy to be back with him once again. There was nothing like coming close to dying to make me realize just how lucky I was to have so much love in my life.

As he led me out of the hospital, he said, "By the way, I had a talk with the chief. Everything's good between him and Grace."

"She doesn't think so," I reminded him.

"He knows he's been a little distant lately, but I shared a bit of wisdom and experience with him, and he's going to do better. I told him how important it was to have someone in your life to love, and to never take them for granted."

"I feel the exact same way," I said as I moved even closer to him, holding onto my husband's arm for dear life.

CHAPTER 18

Five Months Later, Sometime in Late December

"I CAN'T BELIEVE THIS IS REALLY going to happen," Jake said in the early morning hours as he waited for his ride outside the donut shop. Snow had been falling for half an hour, and it appeared that it was going to be our first major storm of the season.

"You're going to have a blast," I said as the first plow approached. Earl popped out of his truck, with his partner Bob not far behind. To my surprise, they weren't alone.

Mayor George Morris grinned as he disembarked as well.

"Are you coming too, Mayor?" Jake asked as I handed out hot coffee and donuts to the men.

"I wouldn't miss it for the world."

"I know I lost the auction, so thanks for making this happen anyway," Jake said as he shook each man's hand.

"Are you kidding? It's the least I could do, since you wouldn't take any other payment for all of your help," the mayor said. "Besides, this sounds like so much fun, I can't wait to tag along myself. Are we ready, gentlemen?"

"Let's go," Bob said with a grin.

All Earl could do was smile, but it was enough.

As the four men took off into the early-morning darkness, the snowfall beginning to intensify, I found myself oddly contented with the world.

They would make the streets of our sleepy little town safe for all.

It was a worthy task, and the four men were more than able to perform it, and do it well.

I watched the trucks disappear, and then I went back into my kitchen, happy to be doing what I loved most, making donuts for my friends, family, and any customers who came my way.

It was a good life, and I was thankful every day for it.

I just hoped that Jake wouldn't want to run the snow-clearing routes every time it snowed once he got a taste for it.

Then again, there were worse ways to spend a morning, and if it made him happy, why not?

RECIPES

A Blast From the Past

This is one of our favorite baked donuts that I make. My family is amazed by how tasty they are, and I used this donut recipe to lead them into being open to trying other baked donuts as I've created them. No one ever suspects that there are mashed potatoes in them! I like to use my mini donut maker for this donut, but I also have molds that are perfect for the oven, and I've used them with great success in the past as well. This donut is rich and thick, offering a hearty treat that's especially good on the long, dark days of winter.

Ingredients

Mixed
- 1 egg, beaten
- 1/2 cup sugar, white granulated
- 1/2 cup mashed potatoes
- 1/4 cup whole milk
- 4 tablespoons butter, melted

Sifted
- 1 cup flour, unbleached all-purpose
- 2 teaspoons baking powder
- 1/2 teaspoon nutmeg
- 1/2 teaspoon cinnamon
- 1/4 teaspoon salt

Directions

Preheat your oven to 365 degrees F, or start your donut maker to the preheating cycle. While you're waiting for the oven to come to the proper heat, in a large bowl, beat the egg thoroughly and add the sugar, mashed potatoes, milk, and butter. Set that aside, and in another bowl, sift together the flour, baking powder, nutmeg, cinnamon, and salt. Slowly add the dry ingredients to the wet, mixing thoroughly as you go.

Grab a cookie dough scoop or a tablespoon and add the dough to your pan or donut maker.

Bake for 9 to 11 minutes or until they are golden brown.

A light vanilla glaze works well with this donut.

Yield: 8 to 12 small donuts

Chocolate Donut Perfection

My family goes through phases of enjoying vanilla, lemon, and cherry, but by far, they always love anything chocolate. This, at least in my mind, is the best chocolate donut I've ever tasted, if I say so myself. They are rich, dense, and decadent. It appears that this book's recipes have the same theme: Pamper your taste buds. These donuts are beautiful, and they fill the house with smells of chocolate that are almost worth making them for the scent alone! I top these with chocolate glaze or vanilla glaze or simply hit them with powdered sugar, but any way you to choose to eat them, you'll be glad that you did!

Ingredients

Dry
- 1 cup flour, unbleached all-purpose
- 1/3 cup unsweetened cocoa powder
- 1 teaspoon baking soda
- 1/4 teaspoon salt

Wet
- 3/4 cup half and half (whole milk, 2 percent, or even 1 percent can be substituted)
- 1 egg, beaten
- 2/3 cup brown sugar (dark for more flavor, light for less)
- 4 tablespoons unsalted butter, melted
- 2 teaspoons vanilla extract
- 1/2 vanilla bean seeds, scraped

Topping
- powdered confectioners' sugar, as needed for dusting the finished donuts

Directions

Preheat your oven to 375 degrees F, or start your donut maker and let it come to temperature. While you're waiting, in a large bowl mix the flour, cocoa powder, baking soda, and salt until well blended. In another, smaller bowl, mix the half and half, beaten egg, brown sugar, melted butter, vanilla extract, and vanilla beans together. Slowly add the wet ingredients to the dry, mixing until it's all incorporated.

In a donut mold, add a tablespoon or more of batter to each form and bake for 5 to 8 minutes. Add the topping of your choice, and enjoy!

Yield: 10 to 12 donuts.

Deep-Fried Peanut Butter Delights

This is one of my first peanut-butter–based donut recipes, and it's still my very favorite. When I get in the mood for something completely different, this is the recipe I turn to. When they are finished, I love adding a chocolate glaze to the top. After all, who can resist the combination of peanut butter and chocolate?

Ingredients

- 1 egg, beaten
- 1/2 cup sugar (white)
- 1/4 cup brown sugar
- 1 cup buttermilk (2% or whole milk will also do)
- 2 tablespoons canola oil
- 1/2 teaspoon vanilla
- 1 cup all-purpose flour
- 1 tablespoon baking powder
- 1/4 teaspoon salt
- 1/2 cup peanut butter (I like chunky, but smooth works fine too)

Directions

Heat enough canola oil on the stovetop to 360 degrees F while you prepare the batter. In a large bowl, beat the egg, and then slowly stir in the sugar. Once it is incorporated, add the milk, oil, and vanilla, stirring as well. Sift in the dry ingredients one at a time, and fold it all into the batter. Add the peanut butter last, mixing it in thoroughly so you get that taste with every bite.

Rake a tablespoon of batter into the fryer when the oil is up to temperature. If the batter doesn't immediately rise to the surface, take a chopstick and gently pry it up from the bottom, being careful not to burn yourself on the hot oil. After 2 minutes, flip the donut balls to the other side if they haven't done it themselves, and fry for another full minute. These times may vary depending on your oil, the amount of batter you use, and the barometric pressure, for all I know! Watch them, and remove them when they turn a nice shade of gold.

For sheer perfection, add a chocolate glaze and enjoy!

Makes 6 to 10 donut rounds, depending on your scoop methods.

If you enjoy Jessica Beck Mysteries and you would like to be notified when the next book is being released, please visit our website at jessicabeckmysteries.net for valuable information about Jessica's books, and sign up for her new-releases-only mail blast.

Your email address will not be shared, sold, bartered, traded, broadcast, or disclosed in any way. There will be no spam from us, just a friendly reminder when the latest book is being released, and of course, you can drop out at any time.

OTHER BOOKS BY JESSICA BECK

45707703R00105

Made in the USA
Middletown, DE
11 July 2017